D.M. JOHNSON

THE DRAGON QUEEN'S SACRIFICE

Edited by Nicole "Cojo" Kralis

First edition

ISBN: 979-8-9950505-1-3

This book was professionally typeset on Reedsy.
Find out more at reedsy.com

To My MOTHER IN LAW Brenda who encouraged me and reminded that I can do this and to never give up. You told me to keep following my dream and I will.

Gone too soon but the kindness and love you have left behind will never be forgotten. I look forward to signs you are popping in and watching over us.

Contents

Preface

Ember never expected freedom—let alone a crown. Born a half-blood and raised as a slave, she's spent her life fighting to survive. But everything changes when a dragon reveals the truth: Ember is the first High Mage in eight thousand years, and the fate of kingdoms rests in her hands. Thrown into a world of magic, dragons, assassination attempts, and ancient prophecies, Ember must learn to trust her power—and her heart. With new friends at her side she is destined to face the Troll King in a battle that could change everything. The question is... Will she rise to the legend she was born to be?

Acknowledgments

I dedicate this book to my childhood Friend Martin Carpenter who got to hear the very first draft of this book,Found Family, the ones who taught me what love really was.
To Irene, the one who took me in when I had nowhere else to go.
To my teachers growing up, thanks for never giving up on me.

To Nicole "Cojo" Kralis who has been an amazing editor.

The Realm of Dragonia

Trigger Warnings

Mentions of Rape no description
Physical Abuse
Child abuse scene.

FOR THE RECORD

There MAY be scenes and words that use derogatory words, slurs, and bullying.

I DO NOT CONDONE ANY BULLYING, HARASSMENT OR ABUSE. SOME SCENES ARE BASED ON WHAT HAPPENS IN THE REAL WORLD TO BRING LIGHT TO CIRCUMSTANCES THAT SOME PEOPLE DO LIVE IN OR HAVE GONE THROUGH.

YOUR MENTAL HEALTH MATTERS. IF THIS WOULD AFFECT YOU PLEASE DO NOT CONTINUE READING THE SCENE EITHER PUT THE BOOK DOWN OR SKIP AHEAD.

NONE OF MY BOOKS HAVE KEY POINTS MIXED IN TO SCENES THAT COULD POTENTIALLY BE TRIGGERING.

Prologue

8000 Years Earlier

Dragonia the realm is ruled by a single king that was chosen by the dwarves, humans and Elven kind. They united under the threat of an evil troll king who sought rule of them and the dragons. The dragons were torn in two, half chose to help and bond with riders of similar personality to to them and joined the realm the other half chose to remain wild in the mountains north of Dragonia. Firelight the first dragon and queen of the wild dragons remained out of the conflict until the troll king tried forcing her daughter to bond with his child. She then bonded with the high mage at that time the troll king managed to kidnap the Queens bonded and disappeared into the Shadowlands home of the trolls.

* * *

Firelight

I beat my wings as fast as I can to get to my Chosen's side. The agony I feel through our bond slows me as I feel the Troll King flaying her alive. The burning pain as a scalding knife slowly cuts away her skin, and suddenly, pain so great sears into my heart as our bond snaps, broken in death. Even though I am at my full size I'm too far away to save her.

Guided by instinct, I land in the Dwarven mountains. With a roar, I blast the side of the mountain with my fire, giving it all I have. Step by step, I tread through the molten rock I create till I reach the heart of the tallest of the three mountains.

I stop as power thrums through me as I peel away the scales on my chest. Slicing through my flesh with my talons, I reach and pull my heart stone from my chest. The human-head-sized ember pulses with its magic.

With a roar, I then bite down, fracturing it into four pieces. As I stare at my now broken Heartstone, I will it to spread across Dragonia. With this act, I seal the future, that a High Mage will have to hunt them down to defeat the troll king.

I fall unconscious as I feel my Heartstone scatters across the land.

Chapter One

King Aragan

I am afraid to even get my hopes up that my wife is pregnant. The chances of conceiving a child after losing your soul when your dragon dies is near impossible. But the steadily rounding of her stomach after a month or so of random sickness caused us to eventually call on the top life-detecting healer. Life-detecting healers are used in battles and for the confirmation of pregnancy.

The healer walks up to Annabelle and me in our quarters. She bows low and then wraps her golden glowing magic around Annabelle's stomach. Suddenly, a rapid heartbeat echoes through the room and off the stone walls. The Healer grins and lets her magic return.

"Your majesty, it is confirmed you are carrying a child and a very healthy one at that!" the healer explains. "I will leave you to each other to celebrate."

I am so excited it's been confirmed by the healers. My queen, Annabelle, is pregnant! Something we never thought would happen due to Annabelle losing her magic and soul when the Troll King shot them down with a poisoned arrow. We are finally going to be parents. I run to Annabelle and scoop her up in my arms and spin around as we laugh and holler, not even waiting for the healer to leave.

"We have so much to prepare for in the next few months!" Annabelle squeals. "Oh, where do we start? Where will the nursery be? What do we even need to get?"

"Slow down, Honey, it's all going to be okay," I tell her. "Go grab some parchment, and we will start a list." She dashes off to the desk that is set under the window. She picks up a thin limestone slab, parchment, quill, and ink jar. She then skips back; her long, starlight-white hair and blue eyes sparkle in the torchlight.

Chuckling, I take the items as she goes to fluff up the goose-down pillows on our grand bed. It has four pillars engraved with dragons and is draped in heavy velvet curtains. We snuggle up, get situated, and title it Baby List. We list things from a crib to a mural for the nursery. We sit there for a bit as we soak in the news of this gift of life. After a bit Annabelle yawned and fell asleep holding the list where she had doodled dragons on a couple corners.

Carefully, I untangle myself and take the items back to the desk and tuck Annabelle in. "I have to go set the guard schedule for tonight," I tell her even though I know she is asleep. Before I leave our chambers, I strap on my saber. It is my favorite style of sword. Its ability to be lightweight, easily handled, and is sharp enough to go through armor like butter. That's what makes it perfect for protection both on and off the field. Walking down the stone hallways that are covered in centuries of hand-woven tapestries of battles, hunts, and families, I am reminded that our own will soon be added.

When I get to the armory where the weapons are stored and the Dragon Guard's schedules and meetings are held, I am faced with a dilemma. I forgot to ask Annabelle if we could double patrols. I so hate making these decisions without her agreement, but now with a child on the way, I cannot afford not to make this executive decision.

"What's up, brother?" Asks Torin, my twin brother, who is seven feet tall and a hulk of an elf. He has brown hair and eyes. He controls earth elemental power.

I pull him into a bear-like hug and say, "You're going to be an uncle."

"What!" he hollers. "That is such amazing news!" He then lets go and jumps up and down with pure excitement.

"After the Troll King killed Starlight, I never thought this day would come," I finally admitted. "Annabelle barely survived the loss of her magic, soul, and dragon." Magic is the life force in our world; without magic, you die. Especially those whose life force is tied to the dragon's Heart Stone when they bond. When a dragon dies, the bonded normally dies instantly also.

"There has to be a reason why," said Torin. "We need to turn to our lore and seek out the wild dragons."

"How? Wild dragons refuse anything to do with our world," I ask. "They live on the Twin Glacier Mountains, and no one can cross that and live to tell the tale."

"It had something to do with the last High Mage. When she died, the Dragon Queen went into hibernation. She hasn't been seen for so long that she is starting to become a legend. She was Starlight's mother. Maybe that's why Annabelle is still alive," replied Torin.

"Maybe. Oh, I wasn't able to consult Annabelle, but I want

guards doubled around the clock now that an heir is on the way," I told my brother as I remembered why I came here. "I hope she isn't upset. She is scary when she's not included in all decisions."

Torin shudders in response. "She probably won't be as long as you don't forget to mention that because of the assassination attempt a year ago it will be needed."

"Extra guards are to be stationed at the two castle entrances, the entrance hall, all four turrets, at least eight, and the wall-walk to have ten guards for each wall. I want dragons stationed at every turret," I command, pointing at each location on the model of our castle. "I also want the fourth-year dragon guard students to start practicing long-distance flights. They will be the ones who are sent with messages to the villages and other territories. We have approximately three months to prepare for the baby's arrival."

"Okay, I will get right to it," Torin said. "Hey, did you know your guard captain also had a child? A boy named Tristan. He has emerald eyes, so we have him on the academy roster already for when he turns thirteen."

"No, I did not; that is amazing news," I answered. "Have him take the next two weeks off so he can bond with the little one and help his wife out."

"He will be grateful," said Torin. "Now, my Highness, you must get your royal butt to bed." He then proceeded to whack my backside with the flat side of his own saber.

I head back the way I came, and halfway there, I bump into my sister, Laura. I tried so hard to ignore her. Alas, it failed. "Aragan, why are you still up?" she asked.

"If you must know, I have doubled the guard, as there is an heir on the way." I reluctantly state. She will eventually find out, so I may as well get it over with.

"That is such amazing news," she gushes as she hops up and down. "I already have so many ideas!"

"Absolutely not," I state. "You are not allowed to touch anything. Annabelle and I have been waiting far too long for this moment. I refuse to let anyone take away Annabelle's joy of decorating and fun." I excuse myself and rush back to Annabelle for the night.

Chapter Two

Queen Annabelle

I wake up and feel excited but extremely sad. This is going to be so hard without Starlight, my dragon. I miss her so much. I know she would be so happy and proud of me for not giving up. I'm glad I didn't either. That day haunts me still. We were off to visit the dwarves for an armor fitting for Starlight when the Troll King from the Shadowlands shot us down with an arrow. It was dipped in Shadow Death poison and pierced her through the eye. It was instantaneous. The arrow went to her brain. I shake off my thoughts and climb out of bed.

Padding over to the desk, I see Aragan has left me a note. *Meet me in the hallway*, it says.

Giggling, I dress and step out, and to my surprise, he is holding a saddle that is way too big for a horse.

"What is that for, my dear?" I ask.

"It's for Vulcan. We are going to the tree nymphs for a surprise," Aragan replies. "Before I forget, with our child on the way, I have doubled the guards."

"You did WHAT!" I yell at him, smacking him on the chest with my gloves. "How dare you do something that I had not been able to ask you to do yet!" I barely hold it together as he backs up with each additional swat.

"Thank goodness," says Aragan as he laughs in relief when he realizes what I had said.

"Why the secrecy about where we're going?" I pout and stomp my foot.

"You will just have to wait, my dear," he answers.

Huffing, I link my arm through his and start dragging him outside in excitement. Laughing, he hastens his steps to keep up. When we emerge outside, Vulcan is lying down by the door, growling at anything that gets near. "Now Vulcan, that is no way to treat our guard. They are here to do a job, and you're interfering with that!" I scold the massive black dragon with blue lightning on his scales. The dragon just nuzzles me in response. Aragan uses magic to put the saddle on Vulcan, and then he secures the various straps.

"We have been practicing something," King Aragan says after he finishes attaching the saddle to Vulcan. "Come stand by his side and crouch a little."

I do as I'm told and squeal as Vulcan picks me up with his tail and sets me thirty feet up and into the saddle. "That is so amazing! Thank you, Vulcan and Honey," I say as I hug Vulcan's neck. Aragan climbs up and wraps his arms around me, holding me secure as Vulcan beats his massive wings. Slow at first; faster and faster we rise into the air. I spread out my arms, balancing as joy and sadness battle for my heart. Vulcan banks left to the west and finds an air current pushing him as we speed along. Sighing, I lean back into Aragan and watch the world pass under us in a blur.

Hours later, Vulcan starts descending towards a forest of wispy, delicate willows. Ever so softly, in a way I had no idea a dragon knew how to, he sets down onto a field of wildflowers of all shapes and colors. The smells of lavender, roses, and lilies permeate the air. A perfume from the land so pure it almost shimmers in the air. Aragan slides down Vulcan's side. Vulcan then picks me up gently with his tail and sets me down in Aragan's waiting arms. Finding my feet, I spin around and take in all the beauty around me. I stop when a willowy figure glides into the field and bows low to me. I nod my head to her in acknowledgment.

"Hello, my queen, I am Bryn Willowbreeze. I am here to help you choose a tree for a cradle and rocking chair that will be sung from," the nymph introduces herself. "Please just call me Bryn. We will sing to the trees and furniture, and items like a bow are given to us by the tree."

"Hello, and thank you so much! This is just the best surprise!" I exclaim, but then somberly say, "How am I supposed to do that, though? For I no longer have any magic."

"There is no need to worry about that. Your heart and that of your child will guide you in this choice. This is because you both take part in choosing the tree. You will both walk through the sacred glade, and your heart and the baby's soul will reach out searching, guiding you to the right tree," Bryn soothes. "We can start as soon as you are grounded and ready. All you need to do is close your eyes and let your feet and soul guide you."

I take a deep breath and exhale slowly, then repeat it a few more times. I take my shoes off, feeling like this will be the best way. Closing my eyes, I feel the lush grasses and ferns tickle them as I slowly walk forward. The grass turns to fuzzy moss as I make my way forward and around a tree. Minutes pass as I walk, feeling a tug on my heart leading me around trees and bends. Never once do I stub my toes. Eventually, the tugging stops, and warmth spreads to me through the ethereal connection I feel. Opening my eyes, I gasp sharply. There in front of me is an enormous willow, towering above into the sky, curling thin branches of leaves of reds and oranges, sweeping towards the ground. Tears flood down my face as I see that the trunk is blackened from fire. By some miracle of the elements, the grand willow still thrives.

Bryn walks up beside me. "There is deep meaning in this tree. I can not tell you why. That day is to come years from now. Just know you can never lose your will to live," she states before she starts singing.

A haunting yet joyful melody comes from her. Sounds from the soul, no words discernible as she sways and weaves her arms through the air. I start swaying and moving, dancing around the tree, eyes closed, adding my own song in. When the last note fades, in front of the tree is a cradle with a matching rocking chair. The cradle is ash-grey with black inlaid swirls and flowers. At the head of the bed is a piece of glowing ember that pulses with light like a heartbeat. The chair matches the cradle minus the stone.

"They are so pretty," I breathe, turning to Aragan, who is wiping tears away.

"Yes, they are," He agrees, utterly in awe. Suddenly, a white light erupts from the tree, glowing as the tree shakes from root to the top branch. When the glow fades, it shows the tree fully healed. Not a burn is left on the grand tree.

Bryn turns to us. "Well, that has never happened before. That set must be protected at all costs," she says.

She places her hands on the cradle and chair as vines wrap around it until no wood is exposed. The vines then wiggle and shift, taking the precious items out of the willow forest. We follow in silence. When we get to Vulcan, I turn to Bryn. "Thank you so much, Bryn. I will treasure these forever," I tell her. "I haven't felt like this since before I lost Starlight."

Bryn replies, "This forest is now healed, all thanks to your heart and the soul of the one you are carrying."

"Thank you so much again. We have to get home before dark." As King Aragan says this, Vulcan lifts me into the saddle.

Aragan then climbs up as Vulcan gently grabs the furniture by the vines. Waving goodbye, we are quickly high in the clouds, headed east to home. By the time we arrive, it's getting dark, and I'm exhausted. Four of the students very carefully carry the cradle and chair to our chambers. We quickly change and crawl into bed for the night. Smiles on our lips as we cuddle and drift off to sleep.

Chapter Three

Troll King

"That child must not be allowed to be born," says the Troll King as he talks into the fire at the bowing silhouette of a woman. "She will be High Mage one day; we cannot let that happen." He turns away from the fire as half his body flickers into a dark gray smog.

I need more time to become whole, He thinks to himself. Half walking, half floating, he makes his way deep underground, where the Queen of Dragons lies hibernating. The massive glowing chains are said to be unbreakable. They hold her down and restrain her in case she wakes up.

When he stops at the giant head of the dragon queen, he prays to the elements that the child will never be born. For if she is, the queen will wake up from her slumber. Satisfied with no signs of waking, he drifts back to his throne.

Chapter Four

King Aragan

This past month has been a whirlwind of activity. Annabelle started painting a mural in the next room, beside our chambers. Twin mountains and dragons flying around it. Some dive, others glide. One is standing on both peaks, breathing fire into the surrounding sky. It is beautiful. That's where I find her, standing on a ladder just finishing painting clouds on the ceiling. "Honey, why in the world are you up there doing this by yourself?" I ask her. I quickly go pick her up and set her safely on the ground.

"How is this more dangerous than riding a dragon?" she pouts.

"Easy. A dragon would never let you fall," I respond with a chuckle. "Now, how do you feel about putting a door between this room and ours?"

"Oh, that is a perfect idea!" she squeals. " I was planning on having the baby in our room till they were much older."

We are soon watching the mason remove brick by brick as

the dragon guard students volunteer, hauling the bricks out in a long assembly line. They pass the bricks one by one. The carpenter then takes a special stick that is nine feet tall and measures and cuts timbers, framing a nine-foot by nine-foot door frame. The two doors are then mounted, marked, and carved with a dragon sleeping in a nest of rocks. When closed, they form a whole dragon.

For the door leading to the hallway, a draw bar is added so no one can access the baby's nursery except through our personal chambers.

Chapter Five

Troll King

The Troll King half-floats down the dark, shadowed tunnels deep under the mountains that make up the Shadowlands. They were once the home of the dwarves. Masters of metalwork and mining. Being half shadow he finds no need for much lighting. He passes cells dug out of stone and earth filled with his twisted, mutilated creatures until he reaches a cavern. Inside the cavern, flickering candles and torches are ensconced in the cracks and crevasses that form natural shelves. Twisted sigils wrap around an altar in the center of the flickering cavern. On the altar rests his son's skeleton. He takes the ashes of Starlight, the dragon that murdered his son during a botched forced bonding, and pours them around the skeleton.

To the right of the altar, a table sits, on which sits unicorn blood and a long knife carved from an Elven femur. In a wrapped braided bundle are the herbs Lilly of the Valley, Angel's Trumpet, and dried Little Apple of Death from the Manchineel

Tree. As well as a candle made from the wax of a fairy comb. In the center of the table is the soul rebirth spell. He reads the spell again for comfort, even though he has it memorized.

Soul Rebirth

Circle the skeleton in the ashes of their murderer for twenty years.
Chop one dried Little Apple of Death
Grind one Angel Trumpet into a fine powder
Mince the Lily of the valley.
Scatter all three herbs over the bones of a loved one.
Then dip the knife carved from an elven femur taken in revenge in
a bowl of Unicorn Blood and splash it on the bones.
When this is done, light the fairy comb candle
and set it on the left side of the skull as you
sacrifice a newly born soul in exchange.

"I will wait however long it takes to bring you back, my boy, The Troll King whispered to the prepared altar.

Chapter Six

Queen Annabelle

I lay down the last fur rug and sit down in the rocking chair in the nursery. Vulcan has been bringing back his food that he catches to be skinned for their hide to be used for the baby. I am pretty sure that he is already obsessed with the baby. He is acting like it's his own clutch. *I can't believe that we have around a fortnight left till you arrive, sweet baby. I am so excited to finally meet you in person. To finally hold you in my arms after all these years of waiting. You are the light of my soul now.* As if hearing my thoughts, kicks rein in my stomach, making me laugh out loud.

"What is so funny, my dear?" Aragan asks as he walks in and kisses my forehead.

"The baby seemed to respond to my thoughts," I answer to Aragan, who then places his hands on my stomach. I watch his eyes light up as he is kicked and jabbed from the other side of the womb.

"That is so amazing, my love," Aragan says. "I cannot wait till this little one arrives."

Chapter Seven

King Aragan

I am so excited but scared. I'm going to be a father in a few days. We just recently announced it for the safety of my best friend and our unborn child. I pull the covers up and snuggle Anna closer. Right as I'm about to sleep, Torin crashes in.

"Wake up," he yells, "an assassin has entered the castle somehow!"

We jolt up. "Anna, Honey, I'm going to send you to the human village, Oakwood Hollows. You will be safe there," I tell her.

"OK, I'll wait for you to pick us up," Annabelle says as we hug. I teleport her as soon as a figure lunges into our room and slices my brother's neck, killing him. Anger boils up as I lash out, extending my hand as lightning snaps and cracks around the assassin, killing him instantly.

"Guards find out where the assassin got in," I bellow. Leaving my chambers, I head to the throne room to wait.

Chapter Seven

* * *

A few days later, right as I'm about to go to Annabelle as she gives birth, a raven flies in with a note.

King Aragan,

I regret to inform you that your child and your queen both died in childbirth.

Mayor of Oakwood Hollows

I collapse in pain and anger. I scream my anguish. I will hold a memorial. I wish I had the time to grieve, but I must figure out who betrayed my kingdom. When I do, they will pay for this. They are the reason I couldn't save the love of my life and unborn child.

Chapter Eight

Queen Annabelle

I pop in front of the mayor's home in Oakwood Hollows, unsteady. I knock on the door in a panic as pain spasms across my back. After what seems like an eternity, the door is finally opened. On the other side is a short human man with blond hair and hazel eyes. "What can I do for you, my lady?" the man asks.

"I'm Queen Annabelle, and I just had an assassination attempt on me. My king teleported me here for safety, but I fear the heir has decided it's time to come now," I answer with gasps.

"Oh dear, come in, come in. I'm Roland Blackwood. Let's get you set up in the guest quarters, and I will run and get the midwife," he says while ushering me in. He leads me to the back of the house to a small room with a small bed and a wardrobe. I settle into the bed, trying to breathe as the pain intensifies.

By the time the mayor comes back, I am holding a squirming little girl crying her lungs out. She has pointy ears, a cute snub of a nose, and all ten fingers and toes. When the little one opens her eyes, I am startled. Her eyes are exactly like the glowing coals of a fire. "Ember, that's your name," I decide, full of joy.

I scream as the mayor rips Ember from my arms and hands her to the midwife. I am then dragged from the bed by Roland Blackwood. He punches me in the face. Blackness becomes my world.

Chapter Nine

Queen Firelight

The sound of a baby's cry echoes in my mind. It calls to me to wake up and find her. A sad voice whispers, "Ember, my child; I love you." Then silence. Moments pass, and I growl in irritation at something heavy weighing on me. Then a sharp scream pierces my mind, jolting me fully awake. I try to lift my head as sleep is still weighing my eyelids down, but I can't.

Forcing my eyes open, I see the giant chains glowing, tying my head down. I roar in rage as my magic lashes out, shattering the chains. Instinct has me up and climbing, clawing at the rock I'm buried under. I sense thousands of years have passed since the loss of my last rider.

Clawing is taking too long. I breathe deeply and release the fire from my maw. Steadily, I turn the rock molten as I climb through a mountain. Breaking free from the top, I view the changed landscape. Darkness has taken over the once beautiful mountain ranges; no sunlight reaches the earth, leaving it barren.

The wailing infant enters my mind, calling me again. I must find her. I turn northwest, drawn in that direction. I extend my wings and fly. Days pass until I come across a little village. Shrinking in size to that of a bat, I descend into a chimney. There in a box is a little babe with eyes the colors of the embers of fire. "I'll be waiting for you, little one, till you come of age," I say to the child. "You mustn't know me till then."

Chapter Ten

Ember

Age 13

It has happened! My powers are awake! I just magically cleaned the laundry. I run to find my master, the mayor, "Master! My powers awoke!" I explain as I slide to a halt. "I was just doing laundry at the river, and it magically cleaned itself!" The mayor turns purple in front of me. *Well, that's a new color,* I think as I backed up, unsure as to why this seems so bad to him.

"You did what!" He screams at me. He raises his hand and backhands me, sending me flying. "You are never to use your powers again! You worthless slave!" I curl up as he kicks me, trying to protect myself.

I do not understand why he is reacting this way. Yes, I'm a slave, but anyone with magic must be reported and sent for training at The Dragon Guard Academy. I bring this up, but it only makes him hit faster. I feel myself losing consciousness as the blows continue to rain down.

Sometime later, I wake up, but I can't tell if I can see. Everything is pitch black. I crawl around to find myself in what feels like a dirt cave. I find a pile of straw and sink into it, blacking out again.

"Slave! Get over here now!" Master yells as he jolts me awake. "You'll never leave this village. This device will prevent you from crossing the river and the edge of the woods. If you do, it will shrink and release a poison to kill you." As the bronze band is attached to my arm, a searing pain erupts from the location as it magically welds itself. I scream. Sobbing, I am then thrown to the back of the cell that was dug out to be my prison. *Maybe if I never use my powers in front of anyone, I will be able to see the sky again,* I think as darkness takes over again.

Over the next few weeks, I am not allowed to leave the house. I find the cell was dug under the back of the house in a sharp-sloping tunnel. When I am out of the cell, I am chained by my ankle to the kitchen floor, or the chain is held by the mayor himself. I am always under watch. I slowly heal. I am too scared to use my magic.

* * *

Age 14

I have to keep my head down and move quickly. It took a year to earn some freedom and get rid of the chains. It feels weird walking without the weight dragging me down physically and mentally. It is a taste of freedom I know I will never fully receive. I learned a year ago that I shouldn't hope for any type of true freedom. Even though the law says I need to go to Dragon Guard Academy, that will never happen. Slavery of humans, elves, and dwarves is illegal in Dragonia. Last year, I found out that for the past twenty years, humans have been secretly enslaving half-bloods. Half-bloods are half human and half Elvin. I am a half-blood.

My mother was human and died when I was born. People would never have known I was a half-blood if it weren't for my cursed pointy ears. Aside from the ears, my eyes are a dead giveaway. My eyes are grey, black, red, and orange. They look like the embers of a fire. Thus, my mother's last word was Ember, which is my name. My hair grew out to match my eyes. These two things are the mark of a mage, someone born with magic flowing through their veins and the potential to bond to a dragon, a dream that will never come true.

Even though it was forbidden for me, I learned to do magic in the dead of night in my cell. When everyone was sleeping. I practiced healing on the mice and rats first, learning to locate my magic in my soul. I learned to speak to the creatures in my mind through my magic. They taught me their anatomy and histories. How to walk unheard and unseen through the dark and even in the day. I use my magic to turn invisible by changing my coloring and clothes to match the shifting colors of the environment around me. I was taught many wondrous things.

One night, I was so hungry that I accidentally teleported my master's dinner from in front of him to me as I was standing in the corner. The smell of the roast and vegetables was too much. I had wished so hard I could have some that with a poof and a crash, it fell to the ground at my feet. Master looked up and slowly stood. "I thought I told you to never do magic again!" He roared as he grabbed me by my hair and dragged me to my cell.

Chapter Ten

I had lain there in the straw on my stomach as the creatures I once healed cleaned my shredded back. The mice ferried me bits of food and acorn caps of water when nothing was brought to me for weeks. During that time, I learned through sheer determination how to tunnel with my magic. If I ever get this enchanted band off me, I want a way to escape. In the darkest depths of my prison hid the entrance to a tunnel. From there, other creatures reached me. Another night, a wolf brought me an eagle that had broken one of its wings when it crashed to the ground during a horribly stormy day. From every cell, tissue, tendon, and bone, I carefully knitted his body whole. When I was done, his wings were made of fire. I sat back, terrified. *I can't do this anymore; he will know it was me,* I silently told the animals. I don't know why the mayor is so against magic, or maybe it is just me. I wish I knew why.

Chapter Eleven

Ember
Age 20

I *finally earned freedom.*

I am by the river where my powers first appeared. Sitting down, I hang my feet over the edge of the bank and kick my feet in the cold water. Giggling, I splash the water, sending droplets into the air. I watch them glimmer and glisten as they arc back down into the river. *Oh, how I wish I could fly through the air. Dipping and diving through the clouds, completely free. To one day feel the wind rushing by, taking all the pain of the past away.*

I am so deep in thought about my past and wishes, that I don't see or hear the flying beast coming until I am snatched up in its claws. The ground falls away at a dizzying speed. It rushes by in a blur as the beast shoots north. For what feels like an hour but is only ten minutes, I am carried in its claws before it drops. Soon, it lands in a clearing of a gigantic forest of towering pine trees. I shoot away as soon as the claws release me and hide around a tree to see what has captured me.

It is a wild dragon. Wild dragons have never mingled with any other race except their own. The dragon is female, shown by the elegant head and the diamond horns curving up and back. The dragon appears to be three hundred feet long and one hundred feet tall. The diamond horns are twelve feet in length. The colors of its scales are the colors of embers, almost matching my eyes. They seem to flicker and glow as the dragon shifts and moves around.

"Ember, please come out from behind the tree. I am not going to eat you if that is what you are thinking." The dragon speaks to me in Dragon Tongue. Dragon Tongue is said orally, but only the person who is bonded to the dragon can understand it and talk back mentally. No one can speak it orally except for me—another thing that marks me as different.

Stepping out from behind the tree, I ask, "Why did you take me? I am a slave, and they will send the village magician after me to capture me and take me back for punishment to remind all other slaves not to try to run away."

The dragon's head rears back in shock when I speak to her in dragon tongue. Then smoke starts to come out of her nose. "How do they track you down?" The dragon asks.

I answer her by rolling up my right sleeve to the shoulder, where a bronze band wraps around my upper arm. The skin around it is marked by livid red and purple veins branching away from it. The bronze band is shrinking slowly in size because of the distance from the village. It also pulses with a black haze as a spell activates the poison throughout the metal. Suddenly, I notice the sweat pouring down my face and the increasing burning feeling of the poison as it enters my veins. I am frightened and look into the dragon's eyes and say to her,

"It's killing me," right before I pass out.

* * *

When I come to, I am still in the clearing, stretched out on my back. When I open my eyes, a giant scaly nose is in my face. Then I remember the dragon. "Please get your nose out of my face," I tell her The nose moves away, and when I sit up, I check my right arm. The bronze band is gone, and in its place is a pink scar circling my arm. In complete and utter shock, mouth gaping, I silently ask, "How did you do it?"

"Dragons have many secrets. This is one of them," she replies. "Before I forget, my name is Queen Firelight of the Wild Dragons. You may call me just Firelight. I knew you were a special person and contained much power, but I thought the rumors that you could speak to an unclaimed dragon were only rumors. I am glad I have chosen you to be my rider. I know only some of what injustice was done to you, for I have kept an eye on you as you have grown, as best I could. Princess, will you accept my offer to be my friend, confidant, and mage?" Firelight asks.

"Why did you call me Princess?" I ask.

At that, the dragon sinks to the ground, bowing her head, and tears drip from her eyes, trickling down her scales. "Didn't anyone tell you your father is the king of the Realm? Your mother was King Aragan's best friend and queen. They were madly in love. When they announced that she was carrying his child, his sister became livid and hired an assassin to murder her. Your father teleported your out of the castle one night just as your uncle Torin was killed right after waking them up. Your mother did die from complications of your birth," informed

Firelight. "Your father has no idea his sister is the one who betrayed the kingdom. Nor that you are alive. We have to catch her hurting you or have her admit it for him to believe she is the one responsible."

"No, I was told my mother was a slave and that she had died in childbirth," I reply in utter shock. I am barely able to believe it, but I have to because dragons do not lie. I collapse to the ground and scream in anguish as I remember every whipping, kick, punch by my master, the mayor of Oakwood Hollow, and his friends doing the unspeakable to me not but a few days ago.

The ground grumbles and starts shaking as my power unleashes, fed by my anger and sorrow. It cracks open behind me as Firelight takes to the air with me in her claws. I am lost in power and anger.

Unsure of the amount of time passing, I am exhausted as I look at the destruction leading back to where we came from. A mile deep, there is an angry gash in the earth. Lava bubbles up from its depths. Firelight follows the path as it leads to the village. I have been held captive since birth. Where my master's home should be is a pit so deep I cannot see where it ends. The village is destroyed. Houses and barns are toppled to the ground like stick forts kids make. The fields and Oak forest are burning down.

I just stare at the devastation until I can regain control of my emotions, scared it will happen again. Firelight looks shocked but strangely proud as she nuzzles my side after we land. "I've never lost control like that before," I mutter. Turning to her, my hand on her giant cheek, I say, "I accept your offer to become your rider. I never want to loose control like that again."

"Awesome! If we get going, we can go to the Tower and unite you with your father by nightfall. Let's leave Oakwood Hollow with what they deserve," Firelight exclaims. Firelight then lifts me to her back with her tail. When I settle in and grab the spike in front of me, Firelight launches into the air with powerful wing beats.

Chapter Twelve

Ember

As we lift off the ground, I get a huge rush of adrenaline. To finally be riding a dragon is truly a dream come true. Each wing beat brings us higher and higher until the trees are just specks on the ground. I can see the curve of the world on the horizon. At each large city we fly over, Firelight flames the air to mark our passing. We pass lakes big and small, mountains small and large enough to touch the clouds that dampen my hair as we fly through them, and forests of all types.

As the day draws close to an end The Tower appears before us on the horizon. Even at thirty miles away, the five lookout towers stretch into the sky. The fifth is the tallest. There is one at each corner and one in the center. The towers and walks are made of solid marble. Red, black, gray, orange, and purple swirl together, and stand out from the lush green prairie that extends for fifteen miles around it in all directions.

Inside the wall, there is a building wrapped around a four-mile perimeter. Stable doors are spaced twenty feet apart. Cobblestone walkways lead from the stables to the tower in the center winding though gardens of every type you could think of. The center tower has at least two thousand openings in it. The rest of the humongous space contains flower gardens. Soaring above are hundreds of dragons doing aerial tricks from corkscrew dives, false collisions, and others with no names.

"The fools," Firelight snorts in disdain at the undignified display of talent. "I'll teach them a thing about the dignity of dragons. I barely have time to grasp the ridge in front of me when she shoots forward at an unbelievable speed that instantly crosses the five miles in a mere five seconds. Firelight shoots straight into the air and begins to grow larger and larger right under me.

"Oh, I forgot to tell you, I wasn't at my true size. I had magically made myself smaller so I could fit by that creek," Firelight tells me when she seems to hear my silent question. She doubles in size.

"How old are you?" I ask Firelight. Dragons never stop growing. The bigger they are the older they are. The oldest bonded dragon known until now was Starlight the queen's fallen dragon, who was hundreds of thousands of years old.

"This isn't my full size, only a mere tenth of my size. I don't really know, as I'm as old as the dragon and troll races my dear, for I was the first dragon that evolved. All dragons are descended from me. Enough talk right now. I must teach my many great-grandchildren a lesson, for they have forgotten the old times."

With a powerful roar that makes the air around me tremble, Firelight orders the dragons to the ground outside the castle walls. Immediately, they obey, for deep in their inherited memories, they remember Firelight. Silently, they land in a fifteen-mile-wide clearing behind the castle in columns that were arranged by size and age. They all lower their heads to the ground as one in a bow as Firelight and I land.

"Why do you frolic around like hatchlings? It is a disgrace to dragon kind for adult dragons to act like that." Firelight speaks so loud that I scream with pain.

"Ember, sorry, dear, I didn't mean to hurt you." Suddenly, a ferocious roar pierces the air.

"Who dares to order the King's Dragon Warriors around?" The voice comes from the center tower, where a dragon stands, all black with blue lightning streaks on its scales. It Is half the size of Firelight.

"I do. I am Queen Firelight of the Wild Dragons, Mother of all Dragons. As of today I am also friend and partner to Ember, the daughter to King Aragon, the lost heir," answers Firelight. As she says this, she lets go of the spell that kept her small and suddenly fills the remaining seven miles of clearing and releases a tornado of fire into the air.

"I beg your pardon, Your Majesty. I had no idea you were still alive, for you have been gone so long, you have become a fairy tale to the young."

"You are forgiven, Vulcan. Please tell King Aragan to come and meet his daughter," Firelight says to Vulcan.

"Firelight, how am I going to get down off of you?" I ask her.

"Oops, sorry, child. Vulcan, will you come over and land on my back so Ember can get to the ground safely? I don't trust those imbeciles you call warriors," answers Firelight.

"Yes, it will be my pleasure," Vulcan replies.

Soon, I am on the ground next to Firelight with Vulcan nuzzling me from head to toe. I crane my neck so far back it starts to hurt to look up at my dragon. I am in awe. *I don't deserve her*, I think.

"Vulcan, who is this monstrous dragon? Why was I commanded to leave a peace treaty with the Lycans? You know how important it was!" A man wearing a jewel-studded crown speaks to Vulcan. The king is six feet eight inches tall. His face has eyes with black irises with lightning blue starbursts in them, black hair, high cheeks, and elven ears. Like mine. He is a mage like me.

"King Aragan, I am Queen Firelight the Mother of all Dragons. I am not monstrous! I am here with your twenty-year-old daughter, Princess Ember!" exclaims Firelight, answering for Vulcan.

"Child, please step away from behind my leg. I'm afraid I might step on you," she tells me softly. Sheepishly, I cautiously walk out from behind the enormous leg into the view of my father.

"Hello, Father," I say to the King. Suddenly, I am tangled in silk robes that smell of pine, and his arms are squeezing the breath out of me. "C-can't breathe," I gasp, for the arms are not the soft muscle of lords but the hard muscle of a miner.

"Sorry," the king apologizes, letting go of me. "You truly are my daughter, for you have Lady Annabelle's mouth and her softly curved nose. You have my height, where she was short, and my long, slim hands. See?" he says as he holds his hand next to mine. To my shock, they are identical down to the tapering nails.

"Your majesty, do forgive my bluntness when I came out here," the king asks Firelight.

"You're forgiven! Now get this child inside and feed her something. She is too thin. Slaves don't get much food, you know," Firelight \ orders the king.

"Hang onto my arm, daughter, and don't let go," King Aragan tells me. As soon as I clutch his arm, he snaps his fingers, and suddenly, we are in the castle kitchen.

Chapter Thirteen

Troll King

When I arrive at Oakwood Hollows, the sight enrages me. I see the cracked open ground that leads to the center of the village. "Where is the mayor, and what the hell happened?" I scream.

The mayor drags himself forward. He's missing his legs. "Forgive me, sire. We had done everything to keep her hidden from the world till you came to collect her. She was always locked up whenever the dragon riders came to pick up the magically gifted," he begs.

"How did this happen?" I ask.

"The slave was over at the river washing clothes when a dragon swooped down and snatched her up." He replies, quivering.

"Then about an hour later, the ground started shaking and cracked open, swallowing the mayor's home, and our buildings were destroyed," a villager states.

"She never was to see the light of day!" I state. "Those were your orders."

With my now regrown body from that battle thousands of years ago, I walk over and grab him by his throat. Lifting him to eye level, I look him in the eyes as I use my clawed hands to rip out his heart.

"I guess I will have to kill her myself." I growl. Tossing him to the side, I mount the griffin I broke and fly home. *Now it is war.* I think to myself. I must gather my forces.

Chapter Fourteen

Ember

The aroma of roast pork, freshly baked bread, chocolate cake, basil, peppercorn, and many other smells make my mouth water, and my always aching stomach growl so loud the king looked at it. "Martha, I have someone to introduce you to," the king calls out.

A door at the end of the huge room opens, and a tiny, round human woman shuffles in carrying the chocolate cake I smelled. Her hair is pure white. Her blue eyes have crow lines from smiling. Her plump cheeks have smears of flour on them. As her eyes see the king, a motherly love fills them.

"Who do you want me to meet, son?" Martha asks.

"It's your granddaughter. She's Annabelle's and I's daughter," the king replies as he takes the cake from her because she is about to drop it. "Her name is Ember, who we thought died with Annabelle."

Tears fall from her eyes as I am folded into flour-covered arms. All this had been happening as if from a distance. Finally,

I break into racking sobs. Years have gone by since I last cried, and now those years of cruelty, pain, and loneliness came in a flood of tears.

When I finally stop crying, Martha states, "You are too thin." She untangles herself from me and moves on, which helps me get my emotions back under control, as I am not used to showing any of my real emotions. My father proceeds to dish up two huge plates of roast pork, mashed potatoes, vegetables, and gravy. King Aragan seats me at a small table in a corner. When I take my first bite of food, the explosion of tastes of garlic, pepper, onion, and other flavors I can't name in my first bite of meat causes me to moan and my eyes to roll back in pure bliss. To finally have something not moldy in so long is overwhelming. Bite after bite I eat, and all too soon the food's gone and my stomach is full for the very first time that I can remember.

"You have the mark of a mage. For some reason, the mother of all dragons, the first dragon ever, has chosen you. A daughter I never dreamed would be alive. When I got the news that Annabelle died bearing a stillborn, I was so grief-stricken. I didn't know what to do. I tore apart the castle to find out who snuck in the assassin. I became bent on torturing even my most trusted advisors to find out who did it. That night I lost you, your mother, and your uncle in a single act of betrayal. To this day I still do not know who did it. Those village folk knew you were my daughter and took advantage of you. I am so sorry. Could you ever forgive me for not double-checking, even when Annabelle's body was never sent to me?" the king asks me.

"Yes, I do because now I have a family where before I had none," I reply. A huge yawn escapes me. I wish I were not so tired because I wanted to get to know my father and grandmother right away.

"Aragan, you had better go back to the Lycans and explain why you vanished in thin air." Martha tells him, "I will put Ember to bed after a hot bath."

"Oh, that would be a clever idea. Night, daughter," he says. He snaps his fingers and disappears.

"Come, Ember. I'll show you to your rooms," Martha tells me. I get up and follow Martha out of the kitchen and into a huge room with a winding staircase. At the top of the stairs is a single door.

Puzzled, I look around, for there are no other doors. "Where are all the doors?" I ask my grandmother.

"There are no other doors. When you go through this door, you will go where you want to go. That way, there is only one exit, and we can keep track of who is coming and going. We moved and redesigned the castle after your mother's assassination attempt and the death of your uncle. The Dragon Guard Academy is now at our old home," she answers. She opens the door after she says, "Ember's Rooms."

With that, we step into a huge room. The room has to be three hundred feet long with the same width. There is a huge opening to the outside, obviously for a dragon. The floor is covered with sand. On both sides, there are five doors each. The first door on the right is a small sitting room with a fireplace and three puffy couches. The second room is a master bedroom with a bed that could fit five people comfortably. It has two fireplaces. The third door contains a walk-in closet that could house nine Clydesdale horses. The fourth room is the bath. It contains a sunken stone bathtub. The fifth door opens onto a veranda with two weatherproof lounge chairs.

On the left, the first door opens to a swimming pool and

heated tub. The second door is a small bedroom. The third door is an identical bathroom to the one on the right. The fourth room is a library with walls twenty feet tall and long, filled with full bookshelves. The fifth room is a storage room.

"Come into the closet and I will take your measurements for gowns, armor, sleepwear, and things for every sort of weather," Martha says. "For the clothes you're wearing, if you even call them clothes, just won't do for the life of a princess."

I look down at my clothes. A sleeveless shirt and skirt made of flour sacks. They are stained with sweat and who knows what else due to the abuse I have sustained over the last twenty years. After five minutes of measurements taken, I am ushered to the bathroom. My clothes are yanked off me. I am about to be plunged into the tub when Martha gasps. "What's the matter?" I ask her as I turn my head to look at her.

"You poor dear! Who could have done this to you?" She replies, for she has seen the scars and fresh whip marks on my back.

"My Master did it for refusing do everything he wanted me to do," I answer. "They don't hurt," I lie.

"Nonsense, stay right there!" She hands me a bathrobe and orders me to put it on. She races out of the bathroom as fast as her plump body will allow her. She soon returns with my father.

"Martha!" I scream, my face turning as red as rubies with fright. "Get him out of here!"

From the main room, there comes an earth-shattering roar.

"Who dares to upset my partner!" Knowing that roar like my own voice, I run out of the bathroom to Firelight. She has reduced her size to fit through the dragon door. I hide behind her huge foreleg.

Martha stammers, "I brought her father so he could heal her back. I didn't know she would be so upset because it was her father."

"I will tend to her hurts, but you stay, Martha." Firelight says, "Aragan, get the hell out of here." The king rushes out the door with concern, love, embarrassment, and sorrow written on his face.

"Now, Ember, what have I told you about hiding behind my legs? There are no men around; no need to fear anymore," Firelight comforts me. "Let me see your back." I cautiously obey. Firelight sticks out a huge, forked tongue and runs it all over my back. Suddenly, I no longer feel pain or any pulling caused by scars. Firelight's saliva not only healed the fresh wounds but also made the scars go away. I look at Martha for her reaction, but she doesn't seem all that amazed.

Seeing me looking at her, she says, "dragon spit heals new and old wounds instantly. Come, time for a scrubbing. That hair's going to take hours to detangle." True to her prediction, three hours later, with my calf-length hair untangled and dressed in silk pajamas, I fall asleep curled up against an already sleeping dragon. I don't feel comfortable sleeping in such a nice bed.

Chapter Fifteen

Ember

"Ember, it's time to get up."

I open my eyes and sit up slowly because I am stiff from sleeping curled into a ball. Yesterday's events come rushing back to me as my eyes drift around and take in my surroundings. I see Firelight looking at me with a softened look that somehow a dragon can make.

"You've been asleep for two days. I put a lock spell on the door so no one would bother you. Unfortunately, no one was able to go to any other room either," Firelight tells me as she noses me into a standing position. "I'd better get out before releasing that spell so Martha won't come at me with her broom like she's promised."

With that, she starts heading to the dragon door, and true to her words, Martha comes charging in with a broom. I explode into laughter as Martha yells at Firelight. She runs after the dragon, swinging her broom. Soon, my laughter is cut off with a groan because my stomach is protesting its emptiness. Before

I can ask for breakfast, Martha drags me into the closet and starts pulling down petticoats and a dress from hangers in a now full closet. *How did these get here?* I wonder.

"Put these on," she orders and leaves the room. I quickly obey, and soon I am dressed. Martha returns with a brush, a comb, and black ribbons.

"Grandma?" I ask.

"What is on your mind, my dear?"

"Why are people so cruel?"

"Most people aren't," she answers. "Sometimes life throws us the hardest things to form the person we are meant to be."

I look down at my once scarred, calloused hands. "Why me? Why did I have to be the one who was beaten and yelled at? Why did I have to have so many people hate me for who I was? I was just a child. Firelight may have taken away the physical scars, but will these mental ones ever go away?" I cry.

"I'm sorry I have to tell you this, but the scars will never go away. In my long life, I learned that those internal scars are what remind us that no matter what, things will change and remind us to keep making good and kind decisions. It is also a reminder that this world still needs some fixing."

"It is a dream come true to have a family finally, but I really don't know how to be a daughter or granddaughter, let alone a freaking princess," I express.

"It will come with time. Dragonia was not built in a day; it will take time for you to heal and recover. One day, you will find someone who loves you for who you are. They will heal the broken heart inside you. Your father and I are here to help you. As long as you are the best you can be, that is all that matters to your father and me. You don't need to be perfect to be loved," Martha says.

Chapter Fifteen

"Grandma, what was Mom like?" I ask. Martha tells me how Mom would laugh at the most awkward of times. How she never seemed completely serious. Her love of horses and butterflies was passed on to me. She talks about how Mom was an amazing painter, and one day she will show me the nursery she painted while pregnant with me.

I tell Grandma about the time I accidentally teleported food from the person who enslaved me, and we chuckle over the face I try mimicking. I also tell her about the critters who would sneak up on me in the middle of the night and how one night they managed to get me a whole cake for my birthday.

An hour later, my hair is done; she shows me to the kitchen and gives me an almost overflowing plate of pancakes and syrup.

"Ember, you're going to have to meet some lords and the king's sister, Laura. Do you know the proper curtsies and mindless court talk?" Martha asks.

After, I prove what I know due to my master, because he has made sure his slaves know how to greet their superiors. She takes me back to the single door, which now opens to the throne room. A long table is set up below the raised thrones on which sits King Aragan, crowned. Two hundred and fifty people turn as one to see who interrupted them. Suddenly, a scaled nose presses into my hand, causing me to look down. Firelight had reduced her size to that of a large dog.

"Ember, let's go meet your father's friends," Firelight speaks aloud.

"You can speak, speak?" I ask.

"Yes, I can. Now do not gape like a fool and square your shoulders," she replies in dragon speech.

"Everyone, I'd like to introduce my long-lost daughter, Ember," King Aragan introduces me. "Come, Ember, sit next to me." He motions to the vacant throne. "You too, Queen Firelight." With a curtsy, I glide across the floor with Firelight by my side. I sit down, and one by one, the Lycan lords and other lords of Dragonia are introduced. Last of all, the king's sister is sitting at a table off to the side. Hate flashes in her eyes. She is identical to the King, but her hair and eyes are a muddy brown and swept up into a bun, and there is a wart is on her right cheek.

"Now everyone is dismissed," says the king. Everyone stands and bows at once to the king and then to me. Each time, I nod my head as court manner dictates.

"Darling, shall we go to the stables for you to choose which horse you are to have?" The king asks. "I bet I know which one you will choose without a doubt."

"Yes!" I practically shout because horses were my friends when I was a slave.

"Then hang onto my arm and hold onto one of Queen Firelight's wings," orders my father.

As soon as I obey, he snaps his fingers, and we instantly arrive outside the stables. "How do you do that?" I ask my father.

"It's quite simple. All you must do is want to be somewhere, and usually you can be there," he answers. "Most of the magically gifted can do this with a sound to activate their magic. Now look around and choose a horse."

Following his order, I go from stall door to stall door. Most of the horses are the average dun and chestnut horses. Some are white and black paints. The last stall is occupied with an orphan foal. It has a coat that matches my hair. That isn't the only strange thing. It has wings. The wings' pure white matches its mane and tail. Downy feathers cover the wings. Opening the stall, I go in. The foal reaches my knee as it stands up.

Chapter Fifteen

"Father, I believe I will choose this little foal!" I exclaim.

"She's not a foal; she is five years old and full-grown," the king tells me. "She has been in here because she attacks almost everyone who goes into the stall. Else she would be allowed into the tower."

Kneeling, I gather the winged horse into my arms and run my hands along her wings. "I'll call you Sparks," I tell her when she nickers. Standing up, I walk out of the stall. Once outside, I put her down and run my hands all over her body. At the base of Sparks's wings, there is a burn the size of my fist. I sense that it is something I can heal. I imagine an ember at my center and pull my magic from it. I guide it flowing through my arms and hands and into the disfigurement. I mentally untangle the tissue and reform the bones, tendons, and ligaments like I had done for an eagle once. When all is normal, I draw my magic back into myself.

"There, now you can fly," I tell Sparks. With a nicker of thanks, Sparks leaps into the air and spreads her wings. Rising above our heads, she performs corkscrews and other aerial acrobatics.

With a sigh of content, I turn to the King. He is staring at me, mouth hanging open and eyes about to pop out of his head. "Why are you looking at me like I just grew troll horns?" I question him. "You look like a three-year-old brought to a sweet shop and told they can have whatever they want."

Composing himself a little, he says, "I had the most skilled healers come, and they couldn't change the deformation. Also, when you did that, fire engulfed you and Sparks, but your clothes aren't even singed. You haven't even collapsed from exhaustion. I am the most powerful mage in the land, and even after healing a cut leaf, I am reaching for a chair. You haven't even been trained in magic, yet you handle your magic like a baker handles bread."

"I have been trained in magic. Just not by humans or elves. I was taught by the woodland creatures, from field mice to the golden eagles. I was taught at night so no one in my village would find out. If they had, I would have been whipped again," I confess. "I can speak to all animals, command the weather, shape change, and create anything out of the air."

As I say this, I show him. I call up a cloud that rains, snows, thunders, and releases lightning. I change my shape to a mouse, deer, eagle, wolf, dragon, griffin, and unicorn. I make a statue of the king rise up out of the ground, made of solid diamond. When I am done, I see that I have attracted quite a crowd! Men in armor lean out of the tower, their dragon heads extending out. The servants gather at the tower's main entrance. Knights line the battlements surrounding the tower.

Turning beet red, I think of my bedroom, and instantly I am there, falling onto the bed. I make a spell that only allows Firelight and Sparks into my rooms. It is one that even the King isn't allowed into. I move to Firelight's room and stand in the dragon's door, watching the scene below. I am soon accompanied by them.

"Child, why didn't you tell me you knew everything there is to know about any and all magic?" Firelight asks me in human speech.

"You never asked," is my reply.

"Why didn't you run away?" she demands.

"It was my only home. I was never allowed to look at maps. I was never allowed to go beyond the creek. I do not know about hunting and gathering food, let alone defending myself from bandits," I answer. "And I didn't know how to break the enchanted armband."

"You're going to have to face them. They were only shocked. There has not been such a powerful mage who hasn't tapped into their dragon partner's magic for thousands of years," Firelight states. "The king is wearing himself out by throwing his magic at your door." With a sigh, I remove the spell and throw up a shield as the door explodes behind me. After the door shatters, the king comes in. I snap my fingers, and the door repairs itself and returns to its frame. I stand and face him.

"Why didn't you tell me you knew how to do so much magic?" the king exclaims.

"You never asked me!" I shout back. Sparks are coming from my fingertips. I hate it when people yell at me. Seeing the sparks, the king takes a step back and fights over his emotions.

When he has control, he apologizes, "I am sorry I yelled. I'm just so used to people telling me everything about themselves; I never thought I would have to ask questions about such an important matter." I let my magic return to my core and forgive him.

"I thought we were alone, and I have never had so much attention given to me. I panicked when I saw everyone." I explain to him. Seeing that he is about to collapse, I create a chair out of the sand and make him sit down. Then I summon up a cup and a bottle of wine from the kitchens. Pouring the wine, I hand a cup to the king, who downs it in three huge gulps.

"I'm going a little crazy with the magic usage because I was never able to use it without being whipped," I tell the king as he eyes the floating wine bottle.

"Vulcan, will you please come and take my father to his chambers, for he is about to faint?" I silently ask the King's dragon.

"I'm coming," comes the reply.

"Firelight and Sparks, you will need to let Vulcan in. Please move aside," I tell them. The winged horse flies into my arms, and my dragon reduces her size to that of a falcon and perches on my shoulder with her tail anchored around my neck. The king's dragon squeezes through the dragon door.

With a flick of my wrist, I levitate the King up onto his dragon's back and put ropes made of magic around the King's waist and around me. I climb up behind the King, and soon we are in the King's chambers at the tipsy top of the tower. Martha is already there waiting. By this time, the sun is setting.

"You leave him here, Ember, and get to bed. You have had a long day," she orders me after I lower a now unconscious King onto his bed. "Put that dress outside your door. In the morning, I will have pants and tunics for you. You might want to save the dresses for formal meetings and balls."

When I look down at the dress, I wince at the mud, straw, and tears. I blush with embarrassment that I did not take care of the wispy cloth. I picture it as it was when I had first put it on. I send a needle and thread made of magic on the tears and force the stains and debris to fall from the fine thread. In a matter of seconds, the dress is just like new.

Grinning, I see my closet in my mind, and in the blink of an eye, I am there. Sparks is waiting for me and pulled the bow at my back that had secured the dress with her teeth. The dress falls away, and Firelight has my nightdress draped over a wing. Crawling into it, I envision my bed and am soon fast asleep in it, with Firelight at my feet and Sparks by my head.

Chapter Sixteen

Ember

I wake up to a feather up my nose. Sneezing, I sit up. The little window in the bedroom looks out on the rising sun. Looking around, I see the source of the feather. Sparks is sleeping on my pillow. She was on her back, wings extended and feet twitching in the air. Laughter explodes out of me at the silly sight, which makes her jump and tumble off the bed. I soften her fall with a pillow made of magic.

Firelight opens one eye and grumbles in protest at the noise. I send the feather that woke me to tickle her nostril, which ends up as a bad idea. Her eyes widen suddenly, and she sneezes. Fire shoots out of her nose and sets the bed on fire. I send a gust of wind that blows out the flames and reverse the damage to the bed with a restoration spell that I trigger with two quick snaps of my fingers.

"Is everything alright in there?" Martha hollers through the door. I open the door and grab for the towering pile of clothes she is carrying that is tipping towards me.

"Yes, everything's fine," I assure her as I hold the clothes that fell into my arms. Firelight reaches up and opens the door for us. Inside the closet, all the dresses are gone except for about ten of them. The dresses are red, gray, and black, patterned cloth. The pile of tunics I had grabbed are the same colors. The pants are midnight black leather that are downy soft. After putting the clothes away, Martha leaves, leaving me to myself. Grabbing a tunic and a pair of pants, I throw them on and take a brush to my hair. Suddenly an idea comes to mind and I put some magic into the brush so that with each stroke, it straightens my hair. Half an hour later, I tie my now floor-length hair into a braid. I slip my feet into soft leather boots that match the pants. My growling stomach reminds me that I need breakfast.

"Let's go get breakfast," I say to Sparks and Firelight. Firelight, still the size of a falcon, takes a position on my shoulder, and Sparks settles into my arms. I open the door to the stairs and step out. As soon as Firelight, Sparks, and I eat, the King comes into the kitchen, talking to an Elvin knight. The knight is six feet, six inches tall. Six inches taller than me, with a well-defined chin, chiseled nose, and his mouth is full and well defined, he is broad-shouldered and he has well-muscled arms. He walks with confidence. His emerald eyes, tense with wariness, flick this way and that. He has a sword at each hip. His belt holds daggers and throwing stars. His black hair is wavy and shoulder-length. His features give evidence that he is twenty years old.

"Ember, I would like to introduce you to your weapons teacher," King Aragan says. "Ember, this is Tristan. Tristan, this is Princess Ember, my daughter. He is a bonded rider to the emerald green dragon Sifron." Tristan bows low from the waist, hands together, the proper bow to a princess. I bow a short way from the waist as royalty bows to the knight. "I am pleased to meet you, Sir Tristan," I greet the knight.

"Likewise, Princess Ember," replies Sir Tristan.

"Ember, why don't you go and get your armor on? Tristan would like to access your abilities in weaponry," King Aragan says.

I imagine Firelight's sleeping chamber and am there at once, walking over to the storage room. I open the door. Inside, there is every kind of armor available, and there are also a hundred different weapons, from spears to swords. A long, separate wall has dragon armor made from crystal diamonds. Having no idea what to do, I silently send a plea out to Firelight. She appears next to me, then flies to a set of armor. The armor is made of tiny links of gold-washed metal. One piece is a tunic I slip over my clothes, and the pants are of the same material. The helmet has soft, absorbent leather on the inside. It fits snugly on my head. Over my boots are solid metal pieces, and for my hands are chain-backed gloves.

"Will you help me put mine on?" Firelight asks. I armor her up piece by piece. This armor can shrink and grow as Firelight manipulates her size. The armor is diamond and gold. When I am done, she perches on my shoulder and helps me choose my sword and bow. The sword has a thin blade and is almost weightless. The hilt of the sword matches Firelight's scales. The bow is a long bow made from oak, and the are the arrows fletched with eagle feathers. Fully armored with a sword at my side and a bow at my back, I cross Firelight's room and walk out the door to the entry hall. When I emerge, there are gasps from below. Gathering by the door to the outside are one thousand armored knights.

"Firelight, you planned this, didn't you?" I silently accuse her.

"Yes, I did. I want everyone here to know you're the King's daughter and my rider. I had us dress in our strongest and nicest armor," she explains referencing her actions. "Now show them what you're made of." With a thought, I am standing by the door next to Sir Tristan.

"Aren't we going to see all that I know?" I ask him. He turns to me, mouth gaping as I open the door and walk through with a chuckling dragon on my shoulder. When I get to the practice field, Sir Tristan and I square off, bowing to each other, and draw our swords. Firelight flies off my shoulders and becomes the size of a warhorse. Then, fast as lightning, Tristan is in front of me. I barely have time to raise my sword and block. I suddenly instinctively know what to do. I spin away and laugh. "So you want me to go all out?"

"Yes, I do, Princess," answers Sir Tristan. For about an hour, we move so fast we are a blur. The only sound is the clanking of swords meeting and sparks falling to the packed dirt. I twist around behind Sir Tristan and put one of his daggers to his neck. He freezes when I whisper "dead" in his ear.

"I thought you didn't know anything about weaponry," he asks me as I return his dagger to his belt.

"I don't. It just came to me as you did that first attack," I counter. Tristan spins as his arms shoot up to grab my shoulders, but I sweep his legs out from under him. I follow with another dagger to his neck. "You're dead again," I state. I execute a back flip as his knees shoot up to ram into my behind.

"Okay, so your instincts are excellent, but your form is absolutely atrocious." Tristan states as he gets up. "It is sheer luck you kept up alone. Don't get cocky again." With that said, my armor drops off my body. All connectors have been sliced. His misses really weren't misses.

Chapter Seventeen

Ember

I am being enrolled in the Dragon Guard Academy by my father because he thinks I need some schooling. Between the weaponry class with Tristan and the fact that I had no "real" schooling in the past, he thinks it is a good idea for the future. I agree with him, it will be nice to be able to do all the things that other people can do!

Firelight flies us to Dragon Fold. That is where the academy stayed after the king moved locations following what happened the night of the assassination attempt. As the sun is setting, the school comes into view. It is a castle with four towers. To the left of the school is a circular arena, but instead of bleachers there are nests built into it with dragons of all sizes resting or grooming each other. The center of the arena is all sand. To the right of the arena is a horse stable and a race track. I don't have enough time to take it in. As Firelight lands, I slide down her shoulder and leg, not waiting for her to grab me with her tail.

I land lightly on my feet in front of the school itself. Tristan and Sifron touch down to the right behind us. "No dragons are allowed in the school building itself," Tristan states. "I'm sorry, Firelight, but rules are rules. We can not give her special treatment if she is supposed to be hiding her identity."

"I don't like this at all." Firelight replies, "I get why we have to, but I dislike the lack of security this place holds. It's been breached one too many times. I will sleep in her room no matter what, though. That you can't stop."

"Now enough of you; we need to go see the Dean." I say, "I will see you in a bit, Firelight." With that, I start walking up the stairs to the entrance.

I push open the massive doors and am bombarded with hoots, hollers, and pounding feet. Children and adults rush this way and that. Clutching papers and dragging trunks on wheels behind them. Some even have collided and are a pile of limbs. There is suddenly too much noise. The world fades to the soft sounds of crackling fire as I struggle to breathe deeply and slowly. Finally, I open my eyes, but everyone is staring at me, well, behind me. I follow their gaze. There is Firelight's head. The only part of her able to fit in the door. She has flames dripping from her mouth like water.

"FIRELIGHT!" I scold. "Put your fire away! I had this. I have to get used to people; you said it yourself!"

"They upset you," she states.

"You cannot just pop in every time I'm upset!" I holler, "I have this under control!"

"Fine, I will try to resist." She responds, nuzzling me.

"I love you; now go find a nest for yourself," I suggest as I pat her cheek. Firelight then withdraws her head and stomps off, grumbling.

"Now we need to go check you in and find your dorm," Tristan says as he ushers me forward. We weave through the halls and wind up in front of an ornate door. Tristan knocks on the door.

"Come in, I have been expecting you, Ember," a woman's voice says. I walk in and see an office with floor-to-ceiling bookshelves. There is a large mahogany desk in the center of the room. Behind the desk sits a woman with silver hair and silver eyes. She looks young, but her eyes look as though they have witnessed centuries. "I am Dean Runa Stormrider. Bonded to the first bonded dragon, Eira Stormscale. So you're the one who had woken the Dragon Queen herself with your cries at birth. It's only fitting you know my true identity. I am tasked with documenting history." Tristan and I just gape as we take this in.

"So, um, how are we going to hide my identity?" I ask.

"Easy. All who already know can not tell anyone who does not know. A spell has already been cast on the names of everyone in the tower who was at the Peace Conference." The dean responds with a wave of her hand. "For now, all you have done is bond with a wild dragon, not unheard of when the dragons haven't found their mates in the wild."

"If we were to change how you two look, people would be suspicious." Tristan inputs. "So, where will her dorm be? I need to be close just in case."

"That depends on who Firelight chooses to nest with. As she will know best."

We walk out to the Colosseum and find Firelight, Sifron, and a purple dragon in the highest nesting room. They are dragging old dirt, leaves, fluffy stuff, bones, and sticks out of the nest. They are kicking them over a ledge and making a mess in front of other dragon nests, causing dragons to roar and flame.

"Firelight, stop it right this instant. What you're doing is absolutely rude," I scold her. "All three of you get down there and clean up."

The purple dragon rushes down and roars at me. I grab its nose and pinch, making the dragon protest. I pull its head down and stare into its eyes. We stare for a few minutes. Finally, it whines an apology as it looks away. "Now go help Firelight and Sifron clean up," I say and point.

"How is she not fried right now?" Dean Runa asks. "That dragon has been a menace."

"Ember is special," Tristan answers with a hint of longing in his voice. "Who is that dragon?"

"He is Imperia; he is one of the more difficult dragons. He keeps turning down potential bonds and has no respect for anyone else," says Dean Runa. "Looks like Firelight has chosen him and Sifron to nest with."

"So where will our rooms be?" I ask.

"You will be on the fifth floor. There is a suite with three rooms, one for each rider. And a communal kitchen." The Dean leads us to the room we will call home. Once we arrive at our suite, we crash in whatever room is in direct line of sight.

Chapter Eighteen

Ember

For the next few weeks, I struggle getting into a routine. Between the classes on learning to read and write and the weapons classes, I am feeling so overwhelmed.

I am not making any progress at all in any of the classes. I legit feel like a failure. I slump through the halls. As kids pass me in the halls laughing and pointing, whispering of the stupid half-breed who doesn't deserve to be bonded. Firelight has been off doing dragon things with Sifron and Imperia. So, I feel even more alone.

Suddenly, a guy with purple hair slams me into a wall, causing my head to crack against it. I'm done with this. This is just too far, so I swing, hitting him in the face with my fist. He tries to hit me back, but I grab his fist, stopping it, and punch him in the gut.

Around us, kids and adults circle, chanting. "Fight! Fight! Fight! Half-breed vs Lycan, who will win?"

This pisses me off even more as I feel the heat of my flames sparking and crackling just under my skin. "If you want to fight, let's go to the Colosseum," I suggest.

Purple hair says, "Let's do it."

With that, I spin around and disappear from the school. I pop up in Firelight's stall. I let go and punch the wall with everything I have. Fire shoots out of my hand, and when my fist connects, the whole Colosseum shakes and groans, which wakes up all the dragons. Now I'm sure I won't kill him. I go to the entrance of Firelight, Sifron, and Imperia's stalls. I stand there and wait as the students stream from the school to the Colosseum. It's time for me to stand up for myself.

Purple and I meet in the center and square off. The dean pops up next to us and says, "No killing, or the king will unleash his fury down on this school. Tap out, vocal surrender, or unconsciousness. No weapons because the removal of limbs isn't allowed. Magic is allowed, though." With that, she pops over to the edge of the sandy pit.

I circle purple, knowing not to stay still for too long. I feint a punch to the left, which he falls for, so I punch him in the shoulder. He grabs my arm and throws me over his shoulder, causing me to land with a thump and wheeze. I spin and trip him up. I jump to my feet and distance myself, knowing wrestling is my weakness. I form a whip of fire. I wait until Purple is on his feet. I flick the whip, which forces him to raise a shield. The shield is made of water. All my whip does is cause the water to hiss as it evaporates. I lob fireballs at him as he responds with water balls. Back and forth we go, sending steam into the air.

Suddenly, it dawns on me that we are on sand. And this isn't going anywhere. As I continue to throw fireballs, I direct heat towards my feet and the area where Purple Hair is bouncing back and forth. Suddenly, he sinks into a pool of molten glass that he instinctively cools. Effectively imprisoning him. I walk up to him and glare down.

Suddenly, a roar goes off, and Imperia shoots down to the Colosseum floor and whips his tail, knocking me away. This leads Firelight to tackle Imperia and clamp her jaws around his neck. She then telepathically speaks to all. "No dragon threatens my rider. Chosen by me, the Queen of the Wild Dragons! You will all respect King Aragan's lost daughter! Your princess!"

"Firelight, I was supposed to remain in hiding for a reason!" I yell at her as I get up off the ground. "Also, please put Imperia down; all he did was bond at the wrong time."

"You're the king's daughter that was rumored to be found alive?" Purple says.

"Yes, I am. I was a slave hidden from the riders all my life till Firelight saved me," I respond as I unstick him from the glass I trapped him in. I grab his wrist to pull him up when I look him in the eyes, and the world fades away. Something snaps between us, and we gasp and look over at the dragons. Was that our fated bond? Firelight and Imperia both bite each other and freeze as water and fire circle them.

The dean walks up to us and says, "One mate bond down, one to go."

"Lord Lin Dire of the Lycans, you will have to move into Princess Ember's suite on the fifth floor."

"You are the reason for peace talks being canceled?" Lin asks me.

"Guilty. I'm still getting used to the whole princess thing," I admit. "It was supposed to remain secret. I was here because the person who tried to assassinate my mother has not been caught yet. And I needed to catch up academically to my peers."

"I am sorry I took my anger out on you because I was sent here to try and bond a dragon. I would rather not be the first Lycan bonded to a dragon," Lord Lin says. "It was part of the peace talks, and I felt like a pawn. But now he is my world. It's staggering to feel that deep connection to something. I also feel a bond to you; it's weird. I get a sense all you ever felt was pain."

Dropping my head, I whisper, "Can we talk about this in private when I am ready?"

"Yes, we can; let's get these two dragons in their nest, and we can go pack up my room," Lin responded.

When we finish putting Lin's stuff in my suite, we head back to the Dean's office. We are both confused as all get out about this bond thing going on. We are laughing about how I turned the sand into glass on him because our magics cancel each other out when I knock on the dean's door. "Come in," she calls through the door.

"So what is up with the dragons and mate bonds?" I blurt out.

"Oh, they mate in threes. One breeding female and one male to hunt and a second who guards the territory." Dean Runa says. "Sometimes the mating affects riders, sometimes it doesn't. There is no way to know, which is why, in my academy, we have suites of three individual rooms. Mate-bonded dragons form teams; they cannot be separated unless by death. This is what happened to your mom's dragon, Starlight, and your dad's dragon, Vulcan. They were bonded; they never met their third mate. So it was just them."

"Ma'am, do I have a say if it affects us?" I ask as my memory brings up the attacks while I was a slave.

"Everything is consensual, Ember; no need to worry. What

happened in the past, you will never have it happen again," Runa responds as she comes up and hugs me. "Lin, while Ember was a slave, unspeakable things were done to her. One day, she may open up about them, but you are one lucky lord. She had taken her initial fury out on the Colosseum walls. You would have been dead if she hadn't." Lin just gulps in response as he pales.

"Don't scare him," I tell Dean Runa, who just chuckles. She has quickly become a parental figure since arriving. "So, who is telling Dad that my cover is blown because of an overprotective dragon? Cause not it!"

"Ugh, why do I always have issues with royalty?" Dean Runa says. "I'll do it. Be prepared to have to interfere, though, if you don't want purple here in chains or dead."

Chapter Nineteen

King Aragan

I arrive livid at Dragon Fold Academy. Cursing Firelight for yelling to the entire academy that Ember is the King's daughter. Now I have to go make an appearance and send guards to the academy to protect her. With the Troll King now active again, sooner or later, he will find out she is alive and will go after her. I head to the Dean's Office and burst in without knocking.

"What in the elements just happened?" I holler at Runa Stormrider.

"A lot," replies Runa, calmly.

"Do explain," I demand.

"One, Ember finally stood up for herself. Two, she whooped Lord Lin Dire's butt. Three, she managed to get the trouble-some purple dragon to bond to Lin. Lastly, Firelight bonded to said purple dragon." Dean Runa answers.

I sink into a chair across her desk and sigh. That is a lot to take in. I lean forward, elbows resting on my knees, as I stare at Runa. I try to take in this information. *How in the heck am I going to protect Ember now?* I stand and walk over to the window. I stare out at all the dragons walking around the Colosseum or flying through the sky as I mull over the dilemma.

"You can send the guards out in training rounds nearby as a cover for protection," Runa suggests as she walks up beside me.

"That is a great idea." I agree. "Now, why the hell did he think it was okay to fight my daughter?"

"It was because he felt like a pawn and was used as a test to see if Lycans can bond to dragons," she responds.

"Well, that's valid to feel that way, but it doesn't excuse the temper tantrum. I have a dragon to see," I say as I watch Firelight, Sifron, and the purple dragon enter the topmost stall. I snap my fingers and poof up in front of the dragon trio.

"FIRELIGHT, WHY IN THE ACTUAL ELEMENTS DID YOU TELL THE ENTIRE SCHOOL WHO EMBER WAS!" I demand as I walk up to her.

"YOU DARE SCOLD ME! YOU ARE A MERE KING, ONLY A FEW HUNDRED YEARS OLD TO MY THOUSANDS!" Firelight thunders back.

"Yes, because you put my daughter at risk. Knowing that the Troll King is your arch-enemy, who will do anything to destroy you. Like he nearly did with the last high mage you bonded with!" I respond. "And don't use the excuse of purple here, hitting Ember with his tail. You know what is at stake. She is not ready yet, let alone be the queen of all dragons' rider."

Firelight heaves a sigh as it registers what she did. The thought of a target on her bonded's back causes her to shrink down and lose some of the glow in her scales. The memory of her last bond rears up. A half-human, half-elf mage, kidnapped and tortured. "I remember that after thousands of years had passed, I was not thinking of the present. If Imperia had struck harder, I feared losing Ember as I once lost my old bond. I panicked," she states.

"I get that, but I trusted you to have a level head here in this school. I know you are the one and only queen of dragons, but I will be having extra dragons and their riders patrolling around the school lands," I say. "I will not risk my daughter getting assassinated."

"That is a great idea," Firelight says, and the other two dragons nod in agreement. "I am deeply sorry, King Aragan, for the risk I have put on Ember's back.

I say goodbye and walk back to the school, thinking about what to say to Ember and Lin. This is quite the dilemma, and I need to plan the mock training carefully to prevent Ember from getting suspicious.

"Dad! You're here already!" Ember exclaims as she opens her dorm door. I peek in and see Tristan pinning Lin to the wall.

"Yes, I am. Now what is going on here?" I ask.

"Tristan won't put Lin down. It's not his fault that Imperia bonded him at the worst possible time," she replies.

"No, it's not, but it was his fault he chose to attack you and thus cause you to challenge him in a duel," I state.

"I truly am sorry for my behavior, my King." Lord Lin says as Tristan drops him on the ground. "I will take whatever punishment you deem fit."

"Hmm, I may have to feed you to Vulcan," I say as my bonded dragon decides at that moment to pop his head to the window and half roars, which ends in a growl.

"Father!" Ember yells, mortified as Lin pales to an ashen color. I burst out laughing, unable to contain myself. They are still kids, so I can't really get mad at them.

"So, on a more serious note, how is school coming along?" I ask Ember.

"Absolutely horrible. I can't seem to catch on at all to any of the lessons. All I was able to do was make my own copy of the Map of Dragonia." Ember admits as she plops down in a chair. "It is useless; I can't read or write. It is impossible."

"I will tutor you, Ember. The Lycans have a different way of teaching that may help you," Lord Lin offers my daughter.

"That is a good idea," I say. "I will not allow you to come home till you can read and write."

"Fine," Ember said as we hugged.

"Now, I need to get back to The Tower, as duty is calling; someone has gone missing," I regretfully state. "I will see you as soon as the semester is done, and I expect progress."

"Okay," Ember says, "Fly home safe."

With that said, I leave her dorm and walk outside through the halls that bring back bittersweet memories of Annabelle. I sneak through a hidden door that hides the old royal chambers and check in on the cradle and chair. I am surprised to see that there is no dust on them at all, and the stones are glowing so bright that they light up the room. Curiosity peaks. I snap my fingers and teleport to the front doors, where Vulcan is standing, waiting for us to head home.

Chapter Twenty

Ember

Over the next month, I truly learn how to read and write. Lord Lin used pictures to help me learn the letters. I learned the ins and outs of spelling and sounding out words. The weapons classes are still my issue; no matter how hard I try, I can't rely on instinct to pass a test for sure. I am stronger and more accurate, but I cannot think my way around a battle. The Dean had to put an enchantment on my armor to stop me from using instinct, which I soon found out was from my past lives as a high mage.

Apparently, Firelight failed to mention she only bonds with one soul, the high mage. There is only one alive every one thousand years. And sometimes the mage is never born due to the Troll King, who is as old as Firelight. He murders the mothers of the high mage. He will not murder a baby who is born, but he will try to kill the woman who will give birth to said high mage. When my mother's dragon was shot down, it was to prevent me from being born this generation.

Chapter Twenty

Dean Runa tells us that the last battle between Firelight and the Troll King happened eight thousand years ago. But because Firelight wasn't bonded, because the Troll King killed her rider, it ended in a stalemate. Both fell but did not die. The king was cut in half, and Firelight fell into a healing hibernation. The Troll King was once confined to a small continent off the shores of Dragonia to the east. Over time, his shadow magic leaked out and took over the old Dwarven territory, forcing the people to abandon the mines and forges for centuries. This was the only way they could escape the evil smog that turned people into evil creatures who ate flesh. That territory is now known as the Shadowlands.

One night after learning of the story, I go to hang out with Firelight and talk. For she and Imperia have not left their nest. "Why haven't you told me anything yet?" I ask her.

"Because, my dear, I didn't mean to rush you; you need to grow and find yourself before the future day happens where we face down the Troll King once and for all." She responds.

"When can I go home to finally bond with my dad? I can read and write now," I ask.

"Soon, dear, now I need you to head back to your dorm," Firelight says. "Lin will walk you there."

I turn towards Lin, who I see waiting at the nest's entrance. When I reach him, I fight the urge to hug him. "It's time you know what my past was like. I also need to explain to you why I put our fated bond on hold." As we walk, I recount the beatings as a child until I turned eighteen. I go on to tell him about how after I turned eighteen, my punishments were attacks, often tied up with enchanted chains that prevented me from using my magic. I tell him that when I fought back, I was whipped within an inch of my life. Then I tell him how the creatures brought me herbs for healing and prevention.

Stopping, I turn to tell him I want to give us a chance when a sharp, agonizing pain stabs into my back. I scream and fall into him. All I hear is him screaming my name. I feel myself being lowered to the ground as dragons flame the skies above, and I fall unconscious.

* * *

Firelight

I watch over Ember and Lin from my nest as they talk, glad to see them growing closer. They stop moving when they both scream. I see Ember fall with an arrow to her back. With a roar, I order all dragons to catch the assassin who shot my rider. I shrink down as I land next to Lin, who has stopped the poisoned arrow from spreading. *"Yank it out,"* I tell him mentally, something mated dragons can do to the other dragon's rider. I drip saliva over the wound. He does as he is told. Soon, the wound will be purified and closed. We just wait.

With a roar, Sifron and Imperia are tossing a screaming figure back and forth between them as they make their way to us. They narrowly miss flaming it multiple times, which I believe is by choice. With a crash, the figure lands beside us, groaning. It is Laura, the King's sister and Ember's aunt.

"Lin, you must go and get Dean Runa and tell her to summon King Aragan. My claws are tied because I can no longer follow Wild Dragon Law," I tell him mentally. He darts off as we guard Ember and trap the traitor.

Chapter Twenty-one

Ember

When I come to, I am in the school infirmary surrounded by people. "What the hell happened?" I ask.

"You were shot in the back by your aunt," answers the dean.

"She tried killing me again?" I ask.

"We didn't believe she could stoop to this level. She is family, but dragons cannot lie. What do you mean again?" my father asked.

"She is the one who tried to assassinate my mother when she was pregnant with me," I reply.

"No, she was so excited for us to finally have a child," the king protests. "I know Laura and I haven't gotten along after the assassin killed our brother, your uncle, that night. The same night, I thought we lost you forever. "

I will bring her here and ask her," I respond.

When she is brought from a cell, the king immediately rushes to her as she walks through the door. "Laura! Tell me you didn't try to kill Ember."

"No, I won't because it was me. I'm the one who was ordered by the Troll King to end this child before she lived." Laura cackles. "The Troll King is the rightful ruler, not you. He is the oldest being alive; he should be ruling, and this mixing of races is abominable. A disgrace. The fact that you lower yourself to loving a human who will only live for about one hundred years, compared to your thousands of years! A disgrace; they are just animals! They should be the ones who wait on us hand and foot. The Troll King will right the wrongs of the land with elves and trolls on top, for he has promised me to be top advisor!"

"I also did it because the crown should have been mine, but our parents did not deem me fit to rule all those years ago. They chose you because you are a man and also had magic. I am the oldest; the crown should be mine!" she says.

"I will take her to the Tower to await trial and testimony by all those here," stated King Aragan. "I may be king, but I am not above the rights of citizens."

"Ember, there is a war brewing for Dragonia. You have been the spark by being the first high mage born in thousands of years. The feud between the dragons and the Troll King has been going on for a very long time. Sadly, you and Firelight are what will keep the Troll King from taking over completely."

Chapter Twenty-two

Troll King

That dang woman failed yet again to kill the princess! *Too bad the king will probably execute her. I had plans to draw out her pain for months till she no longer had an ounce of flesh left,* I think as I pace in my throne room.

It feels so good to have my whole body able to walk and grab stuff again. It has made torturing my subjects that displease me so much easier. At least the dark witches who are gathering up the Trolls, Giants, Zombies (my own creation), Griffins, and so many others have been spared so far. I walk down to the dungeons, cackling at my secret card. Suspended above on a cross frame is the princess's dear mother, Annabelle.

"My queen, I have returned to you," I coo to her. I bury my hand into her shimmering white hair and look into her blue eyes.

"You will never be my king," she spits back. "Only Aragan is the true king!"

"Soon, my child will be born to replace what was taken from

me by that dragon of yours I killed. Oh, what was her name again? Oh yes, Starlight, the only pure white dragon to exist at one time that is always reincarnated as the dragon queen's mother. I've disposed of every clutch the dragon queen has laid to prevent her reincarnation. She will never choose you again. Soon she will never be able to be reincarnated again."

I walk away from her, grinning. Soon, she will give birth to the darkest being in this world. My son. I can feel the darkness in her womb. He calls to me like the other half of my black soul. He will be my child to replace the one that was taken from me when I tried forcing the dragon to claim him instead of Annabelle. The spell *Soul Rebirth* has worked wonderfully.

Chapter Twenty-three

Ember

Two months have passed since I first learned of the war coming. It is now time to hit the skies and become the King's ambassador and gain allies against the Troll King. I will have command of fifty dragon riders, because going by horse would be too slow. The tower is humming with preparations. Since I am going by dragon, I can only pack a few changes of clothes, first aid supplies, and a limited store of weapons. The weapons are daggers, the sword I first dueled with Tristan, the long bow, and a shield matching Firelight's armor, which she will wear. I created a spell that would assemble the armor instantly at three snaps of my finger for her. As for armor for me, I will wear the gold set I first wore.

At last, the day arrives when we set out. It is late fall, and the sky is clear. Birds chirp, and the ten thousand horses have been set loose in the confines of the castle wall to exercise at will. My winged horse trots behind me as I bid farewell to my father and grandmother.

"Please keep in touch with us through Vulcan, and if you need aid, we will send more to you," the king says.

"I will, I promise," I say as Martha smothers me with flour-covered arms. "I'd better get going if we are going to reach the unicorns in three days. Firelight must go slower so she doesn't lose the regiment."

Thus said, I mount Firelight by running up her tail and back and settling myself in the hollow between her shoulders. Sparks settles herself in a special basket with a cover so she will not be left behind. With a mighty thrust of her legs, Firelight lifts into the air enough to flap her leathery wings. Right behind her, forty-seven dragon riders rise into the air. On the left is Lord Lin, my mate on Imperia, one of Firelight's mates. The fiftieth is on her right. It is Tristan. In the past two months, he has gone from a protector to a friend, and I want him to be more than just a friend. As I watch him ride his emerald dragon Sifron, my heart aches knowing it may never happen.

"When are you going to tell him your feelings, Ember? He feels the same for you, according to Sifron," Firelight says to me silently. "It shouldn't be up to the dragons for two riders to do something about their affections for each other."

"Firelight, it's improper for a girl to approach a man like that! The men are supposed to make the first move," I silently scream at her, embarrassed. Firelight's response to that is to flip upside down, sending me from her back. I do not fall far. Once I am clear of the dragons, I turn myself into one.

"Why did you do that?" I ask her in dragon tongue.

"It is because you can't see that he doesn't want to make you uncomfortable with him," is her reply.

Oh, I think, and I forget to keep my wings flapping, so I

suddenly drop like a stone. Firelight appears under me as I turn to my original form again, catching me. As she shoots back up next to Sifron, she orders the dragons to follow as she speeds forward.

"Tristan and Lin," I send mentally through the bond.

"What?" They both answer together.

"When we get to the unicorns' territory, we must leave the others behind. They'll think we are there to attack them." I tell them.

"Okay, that we can do, though they won't like it," Tristan tells me. "How are we going to travel? I can't walk the entire way; it will take months to find them in the Dark Forest."

"You'll have to ride me when I turn into a horse. Don't even argue. Firelight taught Sifron and Imperia the shrinking thing she does so they can follow us," I answer him. "Lin can shift to his wolf form."

Tristan sighs and says, "Okay."

All three days, we never land except to let our riders relieve themselves and stretch. It is noon on the third day when we reach the edge of the unicorns' territory. When Tristan tells the forty-seven riders and dragons they have to stay here, they reluctantly agree to it. I turn myself into a white mare. My mane and eyes stay the same. Tristan leaps on me. Lin transforms into his Wolf form and Firelight Imperia, and Sifron become the size of hawks. Sparks fly above us. I investigate the oak forest and spy an almost invisible trail. With a rear, I plunge into the trees. I lope for hours following the trail. I know once dusk comes, the unicorns will show themselves. With my magic, I am able to sense they are watching us. We finally come to a clearing, and I stop.

"Tristan, please get off. We wait here now," I tell him. As soon as he slides off me, I turn back to my true form. I summon my sword, bow, and armor from the edge of the unicorn's territory and put them on.

"Why did you bring us and not any of the others?" Tristan asks me. My response is to motion at Firelight and Sifron. They are standing on the forest floor side by side with their tails entwined, looking at us. They had waited until I accepted my love for Tristan first.

"That's why. I...," I stammer, blushing. I drop my head and peer up at him. Suddenly, I am in his arms. He lifts my chin so I have to look at him. His eyes are filled with love and happiness because he realizes I chose my heart over fear of being loved. He may not be a soul mate like Lin is, as Lycans always have at least one, but I still love him equally.

Chapter Twenty-four

Troll King

"Come here, my son," I coo as I pick up two month old Salem. He was born the night I finished setting up the soul rebirth spell. He has half my traits and half his mother's, which I despise. Half his hair is pure black; the other half is snow white. One eye is black, the other white, like his hair. He also has mismatched horn colors. His pink lips pull back in a smile, and a set of fangs just like mine are poking through. Soon, he will need blood laced with unicorn magic from the unicorn's horn. I used the last of my horns to create the dark witches. The blood will activate the dark magic locked away inside him. We need to go hunting in Dragonia, where the unicorns have fled. They refused years ago to join my cause.

Carrying him, I enter the throne room to meet with the trolls who will go to hunt with me. Nodding to General Havoc, I permit him to speak.

"We are going to have to take only a handful of our stealthiest trolls for this. Intel the Boa has sent word that Princess Ember is taking a delegation to the unicorns and dwarves to recruit allies," General Havoc states. "She will only take Sir Tristan Lord Lin and the three dragons with her from the border of the Dark Wood Forest."

"How much time do we have?" I ask.

"Three days," he replies.

"We go now; I can't risk leaving my son with the Queen," I order. "Get your men, and I will shadow-portal us."

Going to the armory, I throw on my armor and swaddle Salem in chain mail for some protection. By the time I reach the throne room again, the five trolls are ready. I open a Shadow portal to the unicorn's glade, disgusted by the peace and beauty. I see we are right by the waterfall. With a yell, the trolls charge for the chestnut unicorn lying by the river and pin it down. They stab its side and start collecting the blood, and I walk forward and take my ax and hack off its horn. "This belongs to my son now," I growl at the unicorn.

I look up just in time to see the unicorn queen charging me, and I spin out of the way, holding my still-sleeping child. She misses me but runs through my third in command, killing him instantly. I open a portal back now that I have what I need. We jump back through with the screams from the queen following us.

"Here, my king," Havoc says and hands me the bucket of blood.

"Great job, this blood will work the best coming from the same unicorn," I praise.

I carefully set Salem in the raised basket by my throne and start to prepare the blood. I pour it into a cauldron over the fire and start stirring it with the silver horn. Once the horn touches the blood, it glows, and the magic visibly drains from it in each stir. I continue this until the horn's magic stops flowing. It is done. And ready for Salem. He needs to drink an ounce a day for a month for this to work. I pour some into a mug and slowly feed it to him.

The best part is that in a month or two, the child will be full-grown and his powers will unlock so that he will be ready to begin training.

Chapter Twenty-five

Ember

The ten unicorns sneak up on us, while our arms entwine around each other. Firelight and Sifron are next to us, curled together, and Sparks is flying around our heads, acting like she was the one who brought us together. A snort sends us flying apart. As soon as I see the unicorns, I go down on one knee.

"My name is Princess Ember, Mage Daughter of King Aragan, and Rider of Queen Firelight of the Wild Dragons. This is Sir Tristan Rider of Sifron; Lord Lin rider of Imperia; the winged mare is Sparks. We are here to speak to your Queen on behalf of King Aragan. Could you take us to her? It is a matter that involves the entire Realm of Dragonia," I say to the unicorns.

"Very well, come with us. You might want to return to your horse shape. Your friend will have a long way to walk otherwise," says a unicorn with a golden coat. I return to my horse shape, and Tristan mounts with a small leap. I walk in the center of a line of 10 unicorns with Lin behind me. The unicorns lead us for an hour along a twisting path through the forest at a gallop.

The oaks thin out into a valley with a river flowing down the center and a waterfall at one end. Unicorns were everywhere. Foals frolic alongside mothers grazing on lush clover. The ten unicorns lead us through the valley at a trot to a willow tree next to the waterfall. Underneath the willow is the Queen. She is the whitest of white. She has a glowing horn, blue eyes, a white silk mane, and a tail that flows to brush the ground.

"My Queen, we have brought you, Princess Ember," the golden unicorn says to the unicorn queen. "She wishes to speak to you about something very important." Meanwhile, Tristan slips off my back and goes to one knee. I stay as a horse, unsure of what to do.

"Princess Ember and Lord Lin, please resume your rightful forms," the queen tells us. We obey and bow to her. "Now tell me what this is all about."

"Your majesty, this is a delicate matter. What I am going to tell you will upset many here if they were to overhear it. Is there a place we can go to avoid any discomfort to the other unicorns?" I say to the Queen. "If you wish, we will leave our weapons here." Concerned at this news, the Queen orders us to leave our weapons and leads us to a cave behind the waterfall.

Once the Queen, Tristan, Lin, Firelight, Sparks, Sifron, and I are alone, I put a soundproofing spell on the cave. "You might want to lie down, my Queen, for what we are going to tell you will take quite a while," I say to the Queen. Once everyone is settled, we tell her everything we know of the Troll King's uprising. When all is said, I ask the most important question. "Would you join us in the coming war?"

"I will if you can do one thing for me. Heal my son, for he

was severely injured by a group of trolls," answers the Unicorn Queen.

"Yes, will you take me to him right now?" I answer. The unicorn queen gets up and walks to the back of the cave. She touches her horn to the wall, and a doorway appears to a hidden side cave. I hold my hand up to keep the others from following, and follow the Queen. On the floor, lying on dried grass, is a chestnut-colored unicorn. There is no muscle left on the unicorn, just skin and bones. On the side of the unicorn is a gaping wound oozing blackish pus. He is also missing his horn. I turn to the Queen and say, "Whatever you see, do not interrupt me, especially when fire envelops me and your son; if you do, it will only kill us both."

"Okay," the Queen says. She turns and leaves the side cave, closing the hidden door.

I take off my armor and let my hair out of the tight braid. I sit cross-legged on the ground and place my hand over the wound. Taking a deep breath I reach deep inside to the ember that I imagine contains my magic. I send tendrils out through the unicorn's body to devour the infection that has eaten its body. When that is done, I make the cells grow into muscle from neck to hoof. Slowly, the muscles grow. I then repair the lungs, heart, and other organs. I force blood cells to multiply as I send nourishment to the hair, mane & tail.

The tricky part is the horn. It was sheared off at its base. I form the horn of delicate spiraling bone and then place an ember from inside of me, for the unicorn's magic comes from its horn. Doing this, I know, will weaken me, but the horn is a sacred part of the unicorn. Finally done, I give in to the blackness that calls to me.

Chapter Twenty-five

* * *

I open my eyes, and Tristan and Lin are both holding me. They're looking down at me with tears running down their faces.

"Why are you crying?" I ask them.

"You were dead," Lin gasps.

"No, I wasn't," I tell them. "This happened when I was fifteen and healed an eagle. When I give away a piece of my magic, I weaken and go into a state of limbo." I sit up.

"You scared us so much," Tristan says. "Please warn us next time, okay?"

"I am so sorry. How is the Queen's Son?" I question him.

"I'm right here," a chestnut unicorn answers. I look at it and gasp. His horn is blazing with fire. "I want to thank you for saving my life and giving me the gift of a horn. I am forever in your debt."

"How long was I unconscious?" I ask Tristan.

"A week, but only an hour ago, were we able to touch you and see if you lived," he answers. "You were covered in flames that continued to burn during that entire time."

I suddenly feel the walls closing in. Panicking, the memories of the cell came forward, the dark, dank stench of my own feces. I was forced to live in full force. "I need to get out of here," I say, gasping and shaking as I try to stand up but can't.

"Here, put her on my back, Tristan," the chestnut unicorn says. "I have to show that I live and to publicly thank Ember." Tristan then lifts me on the unicorn's back.

"Oh, I forgot to tell you my name is Charles and my mother's name is Isabelle," Charles says as I grasp some of his mane. Charles goes slowly so I do not fall off. When we enter the main cave, it is empty.

When we emerge from behind the waterfall, the Queen cries, "Charles, my son, you're well again!" When she sees his flaming horn, she gasps. "Ember, you honor us so much by giving him a part of yourself." The Queen comes up and bows to me by curling one leg under her and lowering her head and neck.

"Don't bow. It's the least I could do. A unicorn's honor and being are in its horn." I tell the Queen as I slide into Lin's waiting arms.

Chapter Twenty-six

Ember

In the next week, I recover from the healing of Prince Charles. In that time, I scry my father, King Aragan, and tell him everything that has happened so far. My grandmother Martha yells at me for not sticking to my promise to be careful, and when she finishes, she gives me the recipe to her healing tea. She orders me to drink it as soon as I can. She says it replenishes your magic as well as heals the body.

The night before we are to head to the Dwarven Territory and ask their king for an alliance, Queen Isabel holds a thank-you party for us. Towards the end of the party, Queen Isabel asks us to meet her under the willow tree.

When we arrive, she says, "I can't thank you enough and am forever in your debt. I hope these two gifts will help to pay a little of it. As soon as she finishes speaking, Prince Charles approaches with two winged horses following him. One is a mare and the other a stallion. The mare's coat is of white, pinks, blues, and purples swirled together. Each hair has a shimmery shine, so whenever she moves, it looks as though the swirls flow. The mare's mane, tail, and wings are black with white spots that look like stars. The feathers that cover her petite hooves match her wings. Her body and head are identical to those of Arabian horses. The stallion's coat matches the sky on a stormy day with rolling dark gray clouds with lightning woven in them. His mane, tail, feathered hooves, and wings are the blackest of black with streaks of shiny gold.

"The mare's name is Aurora. She is for you, Ember." The unicorn Queen says. "The stallion's name is Thundercloud. He's for you, Sir Tristan."

"Thank you so much!" I say to the Queen.

"Yes, thank you," Tristan echoes as he scratches his new mount behind its ears.

"You three should retire, for the night has grown old and morning will soon come," Prince Charles comments as he looks at the moon, which is now hovering right above the treetops. "I will take Aurora and Thundercloud back to their stable." We thank the Queen again and head back to the cave behind the waterfall. Soon we are in our bedrolls fast asleep.

In the morning, I sit talking to Firelight. "You should go see if the wild dragons will fight with us," I tell her. "You should take Sifron and Imperia with you."

"That is a good idea. Sifron, Imperia, and I need our own time alone," Firelight says thoughtfully. "For now, you both have two mounts that can also fly, and you can shape-change if you need to transport Lin."

"I think we should send the other dragon riders back to King Aragan. They are only slowing us down," I continue. "They will surely make it so the dwarves don't accept our Alliance. They are an extremely cautious race."

"True. We will do that." Firelight agrees. "When they accept or if you are in any danger, I will bring the wild dragons with me to assist you, and they can carry the dwarves to the tower. I also have to show the wild dragons I have finally accepted a triple mate bond."

"Tristan!" I holler at him. He runs over. I tell him the plan, and he agrees. It was a clever idea.

"We should tell the others and then get going. We have two weeks of traveling to get to the Dwarven capital," he states.

I pause for a second and look at Firelight. "Wait, did you say triple bond? Did your bond click with Sifron?"

She gives me a dragon smile and responds, "Yes, my princess, it did."

With that, we call over Aurora and Thundercloud. Firelight, Imperia, and Sifron bid us farewell and depart for the journey across Dragonia to the Wild Dragon's territory. Sparks is ordered to go home and wait for us there.

Tristan and I ride Thundercloud and Aurora with Lin running alongside in his beautiful black wolf form. He has a white tipped tail, which I find absolutely adorable.

Chapter Twenty-seven

Ember

The first couple of days go without any incidents. On the third day of travel, at lunch, Tristan, Lin, and I are approached by a pack of Wolflings. Wolflings are huge wolves that get seven feet tall at their shoulders. They have always been allies in the past fights with the Troll Kings minions. They help keep them from entering Dragonia from the ground. They also speak the human and Elvin tongues.

"Princess, we need your help," says a Wolfling with brindle fur, that is no doubt the Alpha by his commanding presence that even Lin struggled not to submit to. "My mate has been shot with a poisoned arrow."

"Okay. Take us to her," I say without hesitation, then beckon to Tristan. "Untie Thundercloud & Aurora. They will be safer here; they can meet us when we get to the dwarves. They will know the way."

"Climb on me, and your one man will climb on Silver Frost, my daughter," the brindle wolfling says. When we are on the giant wolves, they speed off into the forest. Five minutes later, we arrive at a huge hill with a cave entrance. "Hop down and hold onto my tail, and I will guide you to my den," the wolf says. "Your mates must stay outside."

"I will be right back after I heal the Luna," I say to Lin and Tristan.

The brindle Wolfling then turns and heads into the cave. Deep in the hillside is a huge cavern. The walls are carved with the wolf's history. From the very first matings, from how mates were found and their battles. Around the cavern are fifty tunnels. The brindle wolfling leads me through the twentieth opening on the right. The tunnel opens to a small chamber with a skylight formed from a tree trunk. In the center of the chamber, lying on a pile of furs, is a pure black wolfling with an arrow sticking up out of its left rib cage.

"Whatever you see, do not interrupt. It may kill your mate if you do." I tell the brindle wolfling.

"Okay. Then I must leave, else my instincts will come forth and I will attack. Just call my name, Russetfur, and I will hear you," Russetfur says and leaves the den.

Now alone, I reach for and draw my magic from within. I send the pulsing energy into the black wolf at the place where the arrow enters her. The arrow was meant to kill the wolf, for it pierced a major artery leading from the heart. The metal arrowhead stopped the artery like a cork in a wine bottle, but the surrounding cells were absorbing the slow-killing poison known as shadow death, which is coating the metal arrowhead. I decide to let my magic flow throughout the body by the veins, capillaries, and the arteries first.

When the blood and every cell are purified, I focus on the arrow. I made an invisible barrier around the arrow shaft so that no blood can leave the artery, which would cause her to bleed out otherwise, but instead only the arrow is able to go through the barrier. Using magic, I ease the tissue surrounding the arrow back so it can be removed without catching on it. Once I remove the deadly arrow, I set to work fixing the physical damage done. I knit the artery back together again. I am finally done when I close the top layer of skin and let the hair grow back. Releasing a huge breath, I open my eyes.

Not again, I think. For once again, I have left a sign of my healing, though this time, instead of a fiery horn, on the side of the wolfling, there is an arrow made of fire on her side. The arrow is made of fur, but it looks and moves like live fire. It also gives off no heat at all but does give off light. *This must only happen to those I save from near death*, I think.

"Russetfur, you can come in now," I call to the wolfling leader. He soon comes barreling through the entrance to his den. "She is sleeping peacefully now. Let her sleep."

Russetfur snarls when he sees the arrow blazing on his mate's side. "What did you do?" He asks with fury and fear in his voice.

"Whenever I save someone from the brink of death, I leave a little bit of myself behind," I answer. "The magic I use to heal is so powerful that it always leaves behind something that shows I healed them. The same thing happened when I saved Prince Charles, Queen Isabel's son. He was attacked by Trolls and his horn was hacked off. I made him a new horn when I healed him, but the horn was flaming."

The black female wolfling had woken up during our exchange and is watching us. "Russetfur, it's okay. Don't be mad at her for something she can't control. It's not her fault she was chosen to be the first high mage in such a long time," she tells Russetfur.

Russetfur nods, "Eclipse, you are right. I shouldn't judge her. Ember, please forgive me."

"You are forgiven," I assure him. "I was wondering if you know of a quicker route to the Dwarf capital."

"Better yet, we have an alliance with them," Russetfur says. "There is a tunnel that leads straight to it. If you'd like, we can take you and your mates there."

When we realize that we will have to ride Eclipse and Russetfur, Tristan pales, so I decide to try the wolfling form and succeed. I have long since accepted the fact that my unusual hair and eyes show up somehow in every form I take.

"Tristan, climb on. We must get going," I tell him.

"Our form suits you, Princess," Eclipse states. Then, she and Russetfur turn down a hidden tunnel. I follow, with Tristan gripping the harness I made so he has something to grip apart from my fur. I ease into a ground-eating lope behind the wolfling couple, with Lin beside me.

At this speed, we will reach the Dwarves in two days, I think. We continue at his pace for the rest of the day until I feel Tristan slump forward as he falls asleep. I gently send ropes from the halter to wrap around him so he won't fall off. Four hours later, he wakes up. I summon bread and a tankard of goat milk with my magic for him to eat.

"Princess, we will soon exit this tunnel into the dwarf's throne room. It would be best if you both were to resume your true form," Russetfur says as he slows to a stop. "I have delegates contacting all races and animals about this war. So as soon as you rally the Dwarves, you head back to King Aragan to welcome them."

"Come. Tristan, you climb onto Russetfur," Eclipse says. "Princess, you will ride on my back." Tristan and I do as we were told, and within minutes of walking, the five of us emerge into a giant room with diamonds, rubies, sapphires, and every type of jewel clustered on the walls.

"What brings you here, Lord Russetfur and Lady Eclipse?" A dwarf sitting on a stone throne asks. He has black hair and a black beard that reaches his knees. He is about three feet tall. His green eyes are framed by a bushy unibrow. He is wearing tempered steel armor inlaid with gold. "We have come with Princess Ember and her mates, the Rider of Sifron, Sir Tristan, and the first Lycan to bond to a dragon, Lord Lin," Russetfur says. "They have come to ask for your alliance with King Aragan. The Troll King is massing an army to take Dragonia and turn it into part of the barren wasteland."

"Then they have come at a great time, for there is a small army of trolls and an unbelievable number of dragons camped just minutes away," the dwarf king says.

"Your highness, the dragons are with us. My dragon is Queen Firelight of the Wild Dragons. I didn't think we would get here so soon because if I hadn't healed Eclipse, we would have arrived a full week later," I tell the Dwarven King. "They are willing to take your army to the tower."

"That's good news," The Dwarf King says. "Now, could these dragons exterminate those trolls? If they do, we will accept the alliance and outfit every dragon with armor."

"I will ask Firelight. Can I call her in here?" I ask. "She can manipulate her size, and so can Sifron and Imperia."

"You may," the king said. I silently call to Firelight, asking her to come to the throne room. A minute later, she comes shooting through the huge entrance doors.

"Ember, you are early," the queen dragon speaks aloud. "I see you have healed another and made friends."

"I have, and I will tell you later. Now, King…" I pause, for I do not know his name.

"Minthorak," the king fills in.

"King Minthorak has a proposal for you," I tell Firelight. The Dwarf King then explains his offer.

"We will do so," Firelight says after she is informed of the negotiation and she quickly leaves.

Chapter Twenty-eight

Troll King

It took far longer than expected to arrive at the Dwarven Territory. Cloaking an army of five hundred trolls for two weeks was challenging due to the wild dragons passing over. There should not have been a reason for this, as wild dragons ignore any fighting going on. Never in history have they done that. I also hate the fact I was forced to bring Annabelle. For some reason, her magic has been coming back. Which should be impossible because I killed her dragon. My son is also with me. He is almost half-grown. And is already starting to manipulate shadows. He is here today to sit off to the side with me to watch the storming of the stronghold doors.

My soldiers finish setting up the tents about a mile from the gates of the Dwarven Castle. *I need to eradicate these tiny vermin that tunnel through the ground like moles. I need to make sure to destroy the forges. Vermin, they may be, but they are the best blacksmiths in the whole world,* I think as I walk through the camp. I enter my tent and sit on the dirt floor.

Chapter Twenty-eight

We need to first blast through the gates…the sounds of whipping wind tear through the camp. Pulled from my thoughts, I bolt out to see an unbelievable amount of wild dragons land between us and the gates.

A small red dragon darts inside for around a half hour, then comes flying out. The dragon roars, "Torch them all!"

In seconds, I portal to my son and his mother at the edge of the trees. I watch as dragon fire of all types, from fire to frost to acid and water, rains down. We slip away through shadows before the flames reach us. Back in my underground fortress, I explode. "For elements' sake, why does this keep happening!"

Chapter Twenty-nine

Ember

The next four weeks are spent making armor for nine hundred dragons. The Dwarven territory is ringing with the clangs of hammers, scrapes of chisels, and the chanting of spells as dwarves create the armor from an endless supply of gems. On the twenty-eighth day, when the final piece of armor is formed and spelled, King Minthorak asks me to bring Lin, Tristan, Firelight, Imperia, Sifron, Sparks, Aurora, and Thundercloud to the throne room. Sparks refused to go home and instead is following along with Aurora and Thundercloud.

"I have noticed that your winged friends require proper armor," King Minthorak says. "For the dragon's help in getting rid of the troll army, I am gifting your friends with our finest armor." With that said, Minthorak claps his hands, and a hundred dwarves file in, each carrying a piece of armor wrapped in silk. "Will you allow us to do the honor of putting it on them?"

"Yes, you may," Tristan and I reply in unison. For Aurora and Thundercloud, there is armor made from a special mix of steel and diamond ore. It is thinner than a sheet of paper and has no decorations, but it has a transparent look to it. Piece by piece, the armor is hooked together and placed on the winged horses. The armor covers every inch of the body and matches each curve exactly. Along the necks, where the manes are, a flexible piece is placed on the neck so the manes can show. When the last piece is latched into place, the armor ripples and smooths into a seamless suit. For their heads is a separate helm made from paper-thin diamonds. The armor changes its color to replicate the wearer's coloring.

Sparks receives an identical suit of armor except for her hooves. For her hooves, there are special shoes that encase each one. The shoes have sharp, narrow spikes extending out to the side. Sifron and Imperia receive an identical suit of armor to Firelight's. Both dragons receive unique armor for their wings. Lava rock has been melted down and then shaped using spells. The spells make the rock move like silk to guarantee maximum flexibility.

"This is some exceptional armor. Our finest armorer couldn't even come close to matching this," Tristan breathes. He is awed by the skill needed to achieve such perfection.

"Thank you for your generosity, King Minthorak," Sifron says and bows his head to the king.

"Now you all have proper armor, and it is time for us to join the main army," the dwarf king says. "I will send three dwarves for each dragon."

"Okay, yeah, that sounds good. You will need to pack a small bag containing two changes of clothes and food for three days," Firelight says. "We will be flying nonstop, so come prepared. King Minthorak, you will be riding my oldest son, Lancythadon."

"You have children?" I ask firelight.

"Dragons choose to have offspring without mating for life. A mate occurs when our interests and hearts align perfectly like that with a chosen rider," Firelight says. "You should go back to the academy after this; you have much to learn still."

"Very well, tell the dragons to assemble by the front gates so the dragons can choose who they wish to carry," King Minthorak says. Within the hour, the dragons have chosen their Dwarven riders and are ready to head west to The Tower.

"My children, please do not perform any aerial moves. If you do, your rider will fall to their death, for you don't have saddles on. We are going to fly in column formation. I want three columns with three hundred dragons each," Firelight says with a spell that increases the volume of her voice so everyone can hear it. "We will be flying nonstop for three days at a steady speed set by me, so no one becomes exhausted. Dwarves climb up your chosen dragon's tail and sit in the hollow between the wings and the neck and hold onto the ridge at the base of the neck and onto each other. Dragons, once the air above you is clear, you are free to become airborne. Once you get into formation, let enough space be around so that when I am half my true size, I can go there if the need arises."

When Firelight is done speaking, I climb into a hollow at the base of her neck. When I tap her to let her know I am situated and that Sparks is in her special basket, she leaps into the air. We are quickly followed by Sifron with Tristan, Imperia with Lin, Aurora, and Thundercloud. Firelight's golden son will fly behind everyone with King Minthorak. If there are any slackers, they will guide them. Soon, all the dragons are in their places. Firelight heads north, staying only five thousand feet above the ground. As we fly over villages, both humans and elves alike race out of their homes to see the strange sight of wild dragons carrying dwarves, accompanied by two flying horses. Before the day turns to dusk, we pass over a field filled with deer and antelope.

As I pass over them, I spot griffins heading our way. I ask my dragon, "Firelight, where did those griffins come from? I thought they lived in the Shadowlands."

"They're coming to join our ranks because the trolls hunt them for their feathers and break them to their will," Firelight answers.

"Okay," I say as the griffins join our ranks and we fly on into the night. Over the next two days, there are pretty much the same occurrences of groups of animals, fae, and humans moving to the tower. On the third morning of the flight, the tower comes into sight on the horizon with a sea of multicolored tents all around it.

"The dragons should land at the edge of the tents. We are going to have to fly ahead with King Minthorak," I think to Firelight.

"I told the others," Firelight states as Lancythadon flies over the wild dragons and settles to my left. Lin, Imperia, Sifron and Tristan are on my right with the two winged horses. The wild dragons land as soon as they get to the edge of the tents. Firelight heads straight for the inside of the wall and lands, followed by the others. Aurora and Thundercloud land and trot to the stable side by side. Tristan, Lin, and I jump from our dragons' backs and then catch King Minthorak as he slides down the side of Firelight's son. Once he is riderless, he leaps into the air to take charge of the wild dragons.

Tristan, Lin, and I walk with the Dwarf King to the tower entrance where a group of people wait. After greetings are done, food is consumed, and a recounting of what has gone on is made, I teleport Tristan, Lin, and me to my bedroom while King Minthorak is shown how to work the unique door in the tower.

Chapter Thirty

Ember

Tristan, Lin, and I are awakened by Sparks, Aurora, and Stormcloud jumping up onto the giant bed with us in the middle of the night. We soon give up getting them off the bed and head for the guest bedroom. This time, we lock the door so they cannot open it, though by the time we exit the door, the winged horses are fast asleep with Sparks. We are jolted out of sleep the final time by shouting in the main bedroom. I rush to see what is going on with Tristan on my heels.

"Martha, you aren't going to get them off that bed until they want to get off. We tried last night. When they jumped onto the bed with us," I tell her.

"Just look at that bedspread," Martha states. I then see the real reason for her distress. It is covered in muddy hoof prints. "Oh, I will take care of it. Why don't you go get some sugar cubes?" I tell her. When I say sugar, the three Pegasuses pop their heads up and nicker.

"I'll be right back," Martha states as soon as she closes the bedroom door.

I burst into laughter. "Did you see how smug those sassy horses looked? "I gasp at Tristan.

Chuckling, Tristan answers, "Yes, I did." Then he calls them over to us using their names. True to the Unicorn Queen's word, they come. Tristan then opens the door and says, "Out!" As soon as they leave, Tristan envelops me in his arms. "I love the way you laugh," he says. "You'd better fix that bedspread."

"It's already done," I tell him.

This makes him look. "So it is," he observes. "Let's go find something to eat."

The kitchen was crowded with people and the Fae. Brownies scurry around, and pixies dart here and there. In the darkest corner, a couple stands sharing a crystal cup containing a dark red liquid that looks suspiciously like blood. In another corner, a Dryad stands over two little seedlings. "Let's grab something and eat on the way to the throne room," I suggest.

So, we grab some egg rolls and bacon and leave the kitchen the ordinary way through the door. The entrance hall is even more crowded than the kitchen. "Okay, let's just eat once we get to the throne room." I teleport us so we arrive right behind the throne. "Hello Father," I say to announce our arrival, causing him to jump.

"Please don't use teleportation to poof into existence behind me," My father states.

"We tried to take the ordinary way, but that was out of the question," I tell him.

"Tristan, where have you been?" He asks. "I was looking all over for you."

"Erm," Tristan blushes. "I was with Princess Ember." The

Elven king turns pink, then red, and finally purple as he looks at us fully for the first time. I take bacon from a single plate, and my hand hovers in front of Tristan's mouth while he is hugging me from behind. "What are you wearing, Ember?" my father asks.

I look down and see that I am wearing Tristan's shirt. Then I look at Tristan. He does not have a shirt on. His abdominal muscles form an eight-pack, and sinewy arms release me. "Martha was yelling because Aurora and Thundercloud stole my bed, and I changed into the closest tunic. I guess I grabbed Tristan's tunic instead of mine," I answer my father.

"Go change into one of the dresses," the king says. I reach for Tristan's hand. "Tristan stays here." My shoulders slump. I obey and disappear, leaving behind Sparks.

When I enter the bathroom, I look at myself in the mirror and groan. My face is streaked with dirt, and my long hair is tangled in a bushy knot. I fill the tub with steaming water and a mountain of bubbles. I go to work, scrubbing every inch of my body so no dirt is left behind. Last, I sent tendrils of magic through my hair to see if I can magically untangle it. Thankfully that works. I then scrub it till it is squeaky clean. When my hair is finally done, I braid a black chain with spikes into it.

I go into my closet and search through the dresses. Way in the back is a black leather dress with chain link sleeves. The skirt part of the dress is cut down the sides at mid-thigh. With the dress, there are black knee-high leather boots and an optional belt that can hold a sword and knives. Finally, when I finish dressing, I pull down a red cape and tie it around my shoulders. I turn just in time to see Lin looking at me like he has never seen me before.

"Hey, where have you been? You weren't in here when we

woke up," I say to him.

"I went for a walk," Lin responds.

"Okay, is everything okay?"

"Yeah, I just needed some fresh air and to take in life before this battle starts. Come on, Princess, let us go save Tristan from the wrath of the King."

We return to find Tristan has also bathed and changed. He chose black fitted pants tucked into knee-high boots with spurs and a black tunic with long sleeves.

The king looks at both of us when I stand beside Tristan and sighs, "Did you two plan to both dress in black?"

"No," we answer together.

"Daughter, you are going to have to wear the emblem of a princess from here on out. Please step forward," King Aragan says. As I kneel before him, he places a black metal circlet on my head. It has a ruby flame that rests on the middle of my forehead. It fits snugly, so it won't jiggle around, no matter how much I move.

"Now, no one can deny that you are my daughter." As I stand up and back away, King Aragan calls Tristan over. "I am granting you the ownership of Rolling Hills Fiefdom, that is where the town that abused Ember is located. You can deal with them as you see fit there. Now you have the title of a Lord, which gives you a high enough station to court and/or marry my daughter if you choose."

"Father!" I squeak, embarrassed at the way he made it so our courtship wouldn't look like a scandal.

"My king, thank you," Tristan says. "I would never hurt your daughter in any way. Thank you for your blessing."

"Now that you both have arrived, we can start for the borderlands where the Troll King's army is waiting. Lord Lin has sent word to his father, and the Lycans will be joining us in this battle," the king proclaims.

"Well, let's spread the word for everyone to pack up and get ready to leave in three days," Tristan says to me.

"Anything else, Father?" I ask King Aragan.

"No, go ahead," he replies. "Russetfur, please accompany them. They must have a chaperon when they are in public. I know they won't be able to ditch you and disappear on us."

"Father!" I protest as the wolfling nudges Tristan and me out of the throne room.

Chapter Thirty-one

Ember

In the next two days, every race and animal seems to get in each other's way, and I have to deal with countless dislocations, sprained joints, heads with goose eggs, and bumps caused by falling poles and tents being disassembled. On the morning of the third day, every recruit is grouped by race and species of animal. The mix of Dwarves, Elves, Dryads, Vampires, Wolflings, Griffons, Lycans, Sprites, wolves, eagles, owls, hawks, humans, unicorns, deer, snakes, and every other unnamed species. The gathered army is spread outward over twenty miles.

I am standing on the roof of the tower with my family while I gape at the support. Sifron and Firelight launch into the air. Their armor glitters in the dawn's first rays of sun. The other dragons, both tame and wild, follow suit. They are riderless because all the dragon riders are going to be mounted on unicorns and horses to guide the troops. King Aragan is going to ride Vulcan because he can easily tell where he needs to send his troops. So, they follow Firelight and Sifron's move but fly over to the amassed troops on foot. Tristan and I mount Aurora and Thundercloud. We are to guide the troops of unicorns and horses.

A tally has been taken of all our allies, and the total is 5 million, from animals to the speaking races. Once Tristan and I reach the front rank, the entire army moves as one east to the Shadowlands. Moving such a huge army takes three weeks. As we journey, we are joined by many more species and races. On the evening of the twenty-first day, we arrive at the borderlands. A natural border of flat, bare slate ground. There waits the Troll King's army of millions of trolls, giants, ogres, wraiths, dark witches, goblins, ghouls, and every imaginable and inconceivable horror from legends told by mother to child.

Dragonia's Army, which is what it has been calling itself, sets up its tents and settles in for the coming battle. As soon as the command tent is set up, King Aragan asks Tristan, Sifron, Firelight, and me to accompany him there. Once the flap is tied, the king blurts, "How in the hell are we going to defeat zombies, ghouls, and the dark witches?"

"Don't worry, I can easily remove the magic of them and send them from this world," I state. "You have forgotten I can do more than save lives with my magic."

"As for the rest of the army, once we take care of it, we will only need to have my grandchildren take care of them," Firelight states.

"If the dragons eliminate all of the army, the rest of our army will be disappointed," Tristan adds in. "Why don't dragons leave the trolls, flightless creatures, and goblins for the others?"

"Good idea," King Aragan says. "Firelight, are the dragons ready to do it now, because then we can hit them when they don't expect it?"

"Yes," she replies.

"Then wait a day or two to let the trolls and goblins settle down and reorganize themselves," he recommends.

"I will go with Firelight so they don't have to worry about the creatures brought by magic," I say. "We will get rid of the dark witches' magic." With that, Firelight and I exit the command tent, and we are soon airborne. Firelight flies high up so I can get the layout of the enemy's army.

Hidden behind a large hill is a sea of black-clothed witches. "Oh no," I gulp.

"Don't worry, I will lend you as much magic as you need to complete this task," Firelight assures me.

"Thanks," I told her. "For everything." With that said, I reach first for my magic and then Firelight's. I imagine the power being drained and sucked out of every magic user in the Troll's Army. I pull and tug and soon have it hovering in a giant sphere.

"What should I do with it?" I ask Firelight.

"Let me take over," she says. "Get back to Tristan and Lin if anything happens, and don't let the other side get my body."

"No, don't sacrifice yourself!" I scream.

"I'm the only one with the power to control this evil magic. Now go!" she roars and tips upside down, sending me tumbling to the earth.

I shape change into a dragon and fly back to our army, circling while constantly watching my friend as she battles with the energy. Breathing a continuous stream of fire as she circles faster and faster, she transforms it into a swirling cyclone. Suddenly, it breaks loose and spreads out and envelops Firelight.

She disappears in the black cloud and flame. Firelight starts to inhale the magic. It starts as a slow stream and quickly turns into a river of black flowing into her maw. When the black energy disappears, a pulse of pure energy radiates out from her, knocking everyone and everything down in its path. Firelight plummets from the sky.

"No!" I scream as I get up and fly as fast as I can to where she landed in the Shadowlands. I change back to my normal form and fling myself onto her head. "Firelight, please don't die."

"Please! I need you! You can't do this to me!" I scream.

I lie there with her and realize she isn't breathing anymore. She is gone. I stay there as all the dragons fly into the air. They all line up in battle formation. Ten dragons fly down and surround Firelight and me. The dragons roar in anger over their fallen queen. With that, the rest of Dragonia's army charges. The battle commences, swords clang, and arrows whistle as they stream close to targets. Screams surround me as I cling to Firelight. Amid the chaos, the Troll King hacks down the dragons guarding Firelight's body. I draw my sword. I parry every blow the Troll King deals. It is all I can do as I have lost my magic. I notice he is slowing, which prompts me to start attacking first. Back and forth the duel carries on until I see an opening and dodge a blow. With both hands on my sword, I scream as I bring it down on his arm. My blade cuts through like a knife through butter. I take his arm.

The troll king punches me, causing me to fly backward like I weigh nothing. As I fly through the air, I see Imperia fly by, and Lin jumps from his back, transforming in mid-air into his wolf form. Lin lands on the troll king and bites down on one of his horns, breaking it in half. He claws at his face and body, and they both fall to the ground. I watch Lin go flying as the

Troll King throws him off him with his feet. Sparks flies in and slices his other arm with her bladed hooves.

All three of us charge. I swing my sword from the side at the troll king's torso, only to meet his sword. Sparks fly with the screech of metal on metal. Lin gets punched to the side as he launches himself at the Troll King, who forms an arm out of his shadow magic. With all my strength and a scream, I duck under his swing as I bring my blade to his knees. With a spurt of black blood, I sever his leg, and he crashes to the ground. The Troll King screams as he gets up, spins, and then runs as shadows replace his leg, conjuring a black cloud and disappearing into it. I collapse next to Firelight in exhaustion and relief that her body remains untouched.

Suddenly, Firelight's body is engulfed in flame. We stand there watching the pyre slowly die until all that is left is diamond armor and ash. Sifron and Imperia let out agonizing roars of deep sadness, and all the dragons shoot fire into the sky. Sifron and Imperia land, and Tristan dismounts and runs to me. I hug Tristan as I cry. We start to place the armor in piles. "Ember!" Lin yells. "Come here."

"What?" I sniffle and walk over to him to where he is digging in the ash.

"Help me," is his reply. So, I helped him dig. "We need to find her heartstone." Suddenly, my hands hit something hard.

"I found something," I say and dig faster. I soon reveal a head-sized oval-shaped sphere that is half white and half black. As soon as I pick up the sphere and place it on my lap, cracks started to appear. The cracks continue to appear until it suddenly falls apart. Two tiny dragons are revealed, each the size of a fist. One is all black, as black as a moonless night in the dead of winter. It is a male because it has no horn nubs yet

The other dragon was as white as new snow with two diamond nubs of horns. The two baby dragons look up and made a purring sound. I am in shock that Firelight had been about to clutch, and a single egg survived and was twins. I keep sitting. Tristan is quicker to recover and continues to search the ashes for Firelight's heart stone.

"NO," he cries, "There isn't one here. How could her heart stone be missing? We will have to search the land for it. For the immense amount of power, it cannot fall into the Troll King's hands," promises Tristan. "Now let's get back to your father."

Chapter Thirty-two

Ember

The weeks following the battle drag on and are so full of chaos. Most of the Troll King's army had fled as soon as he had run away, right after I cut off his arm. Many have fled into Dragonia instead of going back into the Shadowlands.

I trudge through each day like my soul has died. Without Firelight here, everything is dark and shadowed. The weakness of the loss of Firelight and thus my magic, has sucked all the color out of my life. I am sitting with my legs over the edge of Firelight's door, fiddling with a scale that Firelight had shed, which I found buried in the sand.

A loud crash nearly sends me over the edge of the tower. I whip around to see what caused the crash. I see a woman with pure white hair lying there. She is naked and covered head to toe in bruises. Bolting up, I run to her to check on her. She is covered in bruises, and on her wrists are shackles. Seeing that she is breathing, I leave my room.

Chapter Thirty-two

"Father! Come quick!" I scream.

"What is it?" He questions as he poofs into existence beside me.

"A woman teleported in my room!" I yell over my shoulder as I head back to the strange lady. King Aragan follows me and stops in his tracks, gasping.

"That's your mother!" he says as he throws himself to the ground and pulls her into a weeping hug while he directs his magic over her for healing. Slowly, she opens her eyes and cries. Deep soul-wrenching sobs wrack her body. I ease up beside my father and kneel. My mother looks over to me, and we lock eyes. Shock widens her eyes. She throws herself onto me, hugging me. "Ember, I never thought I'd see you ever again!"

About the Author

D.M. Johnson is a wife and mother located in Minnesota. She loves animals. Her love of writing started in Creative Writing class with Mr. Vande Hoef. A couple of poems she wrote were published in some student poetry books and a magazine. It sparked her to start writing fantasy, her favorite genre.

https://www.facebook.com/profile.php?id=61580350024123&mibextid=ZbWKwL

www.ingramcontent.com/pod-product-compliance
Lightning Source LLC
LaVergne TN
LVHW090613110826
845146LV00001B/368

* 9 7 9 8 9 9 5 0 5 0 5 1 3 *